100 Day by Day Stories

Hamlyn
London · New York · Sydney · Toronto

Contents

The snowdrops

Eric and Margaret lived in a pretty farmhouse with a red tiled roof. In front of the farm there was an old orchard.

One day the children's mother came back from the market with a bag full of small, round, brown things like tiny onions.

'What are they?' asked Margaret and Eric together.

'They are bulbs,' Mother told them, but she wouldn't say what kind they were.

Eric and Margaret made little holes in the ground all over the orchard and popped a bulb in each one. Then they covered them up with soil. Not long afterwards the snow came.

'Oh, the poor bulbs,' said Margaret.

'They won't mind the snow,' said Mother. 'It is like a blanket keeping them warm.'

The snow blanket lay on the ground for a long time but at last the end of the winter came and it began to melt. One morning it had all gone but there were still some tiny specks of white in the orchard. Eric and Margaret ran outside to have a look.

'Snowdrops!' they shouted excitedly. And sure enough little clusters of white flowers were growing in all the places where they had planted the bulbs.

The lazy lamb

One spring morning when Robin was walking past Farmer Green's field, he saw that the field was full of sheep.

'All those sheep are ewes,' said Farmer Green. 'Ewes are the mother sheep and soon lots of baby lambs will be born.'

And, sure enough, the next time that Robin went past the field it was full of baby lambs running after their mothers.

Then Robin noticed something far away in the corner of the field. It was a baby lamb, lying down all on its own.

'What a lazy lamb,' thought Robin, as he saw all the other lambs frisking about. And when he met Farmer Green he told him about the lazy lamb.

'A lazy lamb!' said Farmer Green. 'Where is it?' When Robin showed him he said, 'This lamb seems to have lost its mother. We shall have to bottle feed it. Would you like to feed it, Robin?'

'Yes please,' said Robin. So Farmer Green fetched a baby's bottle full of milk and soon the lamb was sucking away happily.

'He was thirsty,' said Robin as the lamb staggered to its feet and began to walk about, 'not lazy!'

The nesting box

'How can we make the birds stay in our garden?' Tommy asked his father one spring day. 'They come here to eat the breadcrumbs but then they always fly away.'

'That's because they have nowhere to nest,' said Tommy's father. 'My trees are too little for birds to nest in.'

'Oh dear,' Tommy said, 'I wish we could think of somewhere for them to nest.'

Tommy's father stood and thought for a while. 'I know what we'll do,' he said suddenly. 'We'll build a nesting box!'

Tommy watched as his father made a little house with a wooden roof and a round hole in the front. When it was ready, Tommy's father climbed a ladder and fixed the little nesting box securely on to the wall.

For days and days they watched to see if any birds would go into their new house.

Then one day a little bluetit flew straight into the house and chirruped eagerly to its mate. Then the two bluetits worked busily with bits of moss and odds and ends until their nest was complete.

'Now we have some birds who stay in our garden,' said Tommy.

The slide

'What cold, frosty weather for early spring,' said Mum to Jan. 'I hope the paths aren't all slippery when we go to the shops.'

But the paths *were* slippery and, when Mum stopped to talk to her friend Mrs Brown, Jan managed to make six slides in a row on all the slippery patches. 'Sliding is fun,' she said.

But Mum said, 'I hope the sun comes out as soon as possible and melts it all.'

When they got near the shops, Jan met Peter from next door. 'I've made a really big slide over there,' he said. 'Come and have a go on it.'

'Oh dear,' said Mum when she saw all the children racing up and down on the icy pavement, making it more and more slippery, 'I hope no one falls over and gets hurt.'

While Mum was in the supermarket, Jan had a go on the big long slide. It shone like an icy mirror and at first she only did a very small, wobbly slither. But soon she could slide all the way along.

Then she said to Peter and the other children, 'I'm just going into the sweet shop.'

The sweet shop had all sorts of sweets in big glass bottles. Jan asked for some jelly-babies, and the shop-lady tipped out some and put them in a paper bag.

Then Jan ran out to give all the others a jelly-baby. But, whoosh . . . she ran right on to the long slide, and whizz . . . the sweets flew in the air and the bag burst, scattering the jelly-babies all over the ground. And plonk . . . Jan bumped right into a man with a big shovel!

'What do you think you're doing, young lady?' he said. Then he asked, 'Why don't you children help me to spread this salted grit about to keep the paths safe for people?' And he threw a big shovelful of grit on to the slide, and the children gave a huge groan.

'Our slide has gone,' said everyone sadly.

Then suddenly the sun came out and all the slippery patches melted away.

'A lovely spring day at last!' said Mum when she came out of the supermarket. 'And there will be no more ice until next year – thank goodness!'

The wind

The wind in spring is a busy wind. It has to blow away all the old bits and pieces that belong to winter and make the land ready for spring. It isn't a cold wind, for it needs to warm the ground, but it isn't a soft wind either. It is very strong. It wakes everything up.

First the busy wind blows into the woods, scattering last year's dead leaves and pushing them to one side. It unblocks the holes where the creatures are hiding. 'Come out. Get about. Spring is here,' it calls down their holes.

Then it blows hard against the trees, tugging angrily at the old brown leaves left clinging to the branches. It breaks off small dead twigs for the birds to pick up to build their new nests. 'Stop resting. Get nesting,' it calls to the birds.

Next the warm wind blows over the fields, melting the last patches of winter snow. As it blows it calls down to the seeds, 'Start to grow. There's no more snow.'

Finally, when the spring wind is satisfied it has completed its work, it blows itself right away.

Carnival!

Helmut and Ingrid were very excited. Soon it would be Carnival time. In Germany, where they lived, everyone celebrates the end of the winter. There is dancing and feasting. Brass bands play in the streets and there are processions where everyone wears fancy-dress costumes.

Helmut's mother had made him a teddy-bear costume out of an old fur coat. She had made him a mask with a big smiling mouth and floppy ears.

Ingrid was going dressed as a sunflower. Mother had covered one of Ingrid's dresses with yellow crepe-paper petals. She had made her a bonnet covered with petals, too, and a tiny petal mask.

At last it was the day of the Carnival.

'Oompah, oompah, boom, boom!' Helmut and Ingrid heard the sound of the band approaching.

'Come on,' called Helmut and together they ran and joined the procession. Their friends were already there – one dressed as a mouse, another as a fairy, another as a pirate. Coloured paper streamers and balloons floated through the air. Everyone was singing and dancing.

'Hurrah!' shouted Helmut and Ingrid. 'Hurrah for Carnival!'

The sticky buds

Billy was sending a birthday card to his gran. Her birthday was in the spring and he had chosen a lovely card covered in flowers.

'I will write Gran's address on some paper. Then you can copy it on to the envelope,' said Billy's mum.

Billy was excited. It was the first time he had written an address on an envelope.

'Very good, dear,' smiled Mum when he'd finished. 'Now you will need to seal it up. Lick the flap on the back of the envelope and stick it down.'

So Billy licked the envelope flap very, very well, and then he pressed it down.

But it came undone!

'You've licked it so well you've licked all the sticky-stuff off,' said Mum laughing.

Just then Billy's sister Beverley came in holding some twigs with big brownish green buds on. The buds looked as if they'd been dipped in a treacle pot!

'They're sticky buds,' said Beverley. 'When they open up, they will grow into beautiful little horse chestnut leaves.'

Beverley put the buds down on the table and she and Mum went to find a vase to put them in.

'I wonder if they'll stick this envelope flap,' said Billy touching the sticky buds. 'They feel very sticky.' And Billy rubbed one of the buds against the envelope.

But no, still the flap came undone and the bud left a nasty, sticky, brown mark on the envelope!

When Mum came back and saw what Billy had done, she said, 'That was a good idea Billy, but I'm afraid sticky buds can't really be used instead of glue! You'll have to write another envelope for Gran's card.'

17

The dolphin

When Jane went to the seaside to see Gran and Grandad she took her swimsuit.

'I'm afraid the sea's a bit too cold for swimming or even paddling in at the moment,' said Grandad, 'but we could go for a walk along the beach.'

'Can we take your binoculars, please?' asked Jane. She loved the binoculars. They were like big black tunnels that you held up to your eyes and looked through. And they made things that were small and a long way off look big and very near.

'What would you like to see through my binoculars?' asked Grandad, smiling.

'A dolphin like the one I saw at the zoo,' said Jane. 'But I'd like to see one swimming in the real sea.'

'We aren't likely to see many dolphins along this coast,' said Grandad. 'But we might see a ship.'

So they set off and soon they came to a very rocky cliff high above the sea.

'We can sit here and look out to sea,' said Grandad. Then he said, 'I think I can see a boat a long way off.' And he told Jane to look through the binoculars.

'Whatever it is keeps leaping up out of the sea – then disappearing!' laughed Jane. 'It can't be a boat. It's getting nearer and nearer. I can see it without the binoculars now. It's playing a game! It's a dolphin!' Jane cried. And she waved to it and shouted, 'Hello dolphin!'

The dolphin leapt in the air again and almost seemed to wave its flippers at them before it swam away out to sea.

'What a surprising sight,' said Grandad. 'He must have known we were waiting to see him.'

'I wish the sea was warm enough for me to learn to swim like a dolphin,' said Jane when they got home and she had told Gran all about their adventure.

'You *can* learn to swim like a dolphin,' smiled Gran. 'This afternoon we'll all go to the swimming baths and you can have a swimming lesson.'

Archibald the frog

Archibald the frog was very lonely. It was spring, and he wanted to settle down with a beautiful lady frog and have lots and lots of frogspawn which would hatch out into lots and lots of tadpoles which would grow into lots and lots of baby frogs. He closed his eyes and fell into a dream. He dreamt about a beautiful green lady frog and lots and lots of wriggly black tadpoles growing into lots and lots of bright green baby frogs.

Archibald heard a croak and opened his eyes, and there, right in front of him, was the most beautiful lady frog. Archibald couldn't believe his eyes so he shut them again tightly, croaked, and re-opened them. She was still there.

'Hello,' she croaked.

Soon Archibald was the happiest frog in all the land because everything he had dreamed about came true. The beautiful lady frog stayed with him and laid lots and lots of frogspawn. Later in spring the little black specks in the frogspawn jelly hatched out into little wriggly black tadpoles. There were exactly two hundred and fifty-three tadpoles.

'Oh dear,' said Mrs Archibald. 'It's all very well you looking so pleased with yourself Archibald dear, but whatever shall we call them all? Can you think of two hundred and fifty-three names?'

Archibald couldn't. Can you?

The beech leaves

Karl lived on the edge of a small town in Denmark. Not far away from his home was a large beech wood. Karl and his brothers and sisters liked to go for walks in the wood.

Karl liked it in autumn when the leaves on the trees turned a beautiful golden colour. He liked it in winter, too. Then he made patterns in the snow with his footprints.

But one year the winter lasted a long, long time. There was snow and frost and rain and fog. The children could not go to the wood then.

But at last the winter was over. One morning when the sun was shining a little, Mother said to the children, 'Today we are going to the beech wood to look for the spring.'

'Hurray!' shouted Karl and his brothers and sisters. This was the day they had been waiting for.

When they got to the wood the children gathered small branches of shiny green beech leaves.

'Spring has come back,' said Mother. 'Now we will take the leaves home to decorate the house.'

'Welcome, spring, welcome!' sang Karl as he walked home holding the leaves high above his head.

Dilly the dormouse

Right in the middle of a cornfield, right in the centre of a burrow, right in the heart of a nest made of feathers, moss, leaves and straw, Dilly the dormouse was curled up fast asleep. All through the winter Dilly lay sleeping; her paws and nose curled tightly inwards. But she left her tail sticking out of the nest – that never felt the cold.

One day in spring when the sun had melted the ice and snow and the new things began to grow, a small shaft of sunlight found its way into the burrow and touched the tip of Dilly's tail. The tail twitched and woke her up. She yawned, uncurled, and poked her head out of the nest. Then she cleaned her whiskers and tried to open her eyes. But it was no good. 'I'm far too sleepy to open my eyes,' she said. 'I'm going back to sleep.' So she did.

Two days later, when the sun shone again, it sent another shaft of light down the burrow. It warmed up Dilly's tail so much that it wriggled. This time she yawned, uncurled, poked her head out of the nest, cleaned her whiskers, stretched as long as she could and opened her eyes. 'Oh it's far too bright. I'm terribly, terribly sleepy. I'm going back to bed.' And so she did.

During the night, Dilly's stomach began to rumble, and
she felt so hungry that she awoke before dawn. She yawned,
uncurled, poked her nose out of her nest, washed her
whiskers and opened her eyes. It was still dark as she made
her way up the burrow. At the top she poked out her nose
and smelt for danger. All she could sniff was the warm air
and the smells of freshly growing plants. Quietly she sat until
the dawn broke, and there in front of her was the outside
world. It was golden and yellow and green and brown with
a blue sky and white clouds. And she saw in front of her
lots of good things to nibble at.

'It's spring,' she squeaked. 'How happy I am.'

The spring blossom

Pedro and Maria Gonzalez lived on a farm in Spain. The Gonzalez family were very proud of their farm. They had a fine cockerel that crowed loudly in the morning, lots of hens who laid lots of eggs, two goats that gave them milk and ate the grass in the orchard and a sand-coloured dog called Hugo who barked if anyone came to the farm. But most important of all was their almond orchard, for the almonds they gathered and sold in the autumn provided enough money to keep the Gonzalez family for the whole year.

Pedro and Maria found it hard work harvesting the almonds. They preferred the spring. In spring something wonderful happened to the almond trees. They burst into a mass of pale pink blossom. Then Maria and Pedro would run up the avenues of trees shouting and singing and playing in the fallen blossom.

One spring, Mr and Mrs Gonzalez stood watching the children playing in the orchard. It was as if they were playing in pink snowflakes. Suddenly Mrs Gonzalez looked at her husband and said, 'Let's go and play in the blossoms too and pretend we are young again.'

Mr Gonzalez laughed and said, 'Better still – the whole farm shall play.'

They ran into the farmyard, and while Mr Gonzalez fetched the two goats, Mrs Gonzalez and Hugo the dog rounded up the cockerel and chickens and drove them all into the orchard. Pedro and Maria were surprised! They weren't expecting this to happen!

The cockerel and the chickens scuffed up the petals with their beaks and wings so that pink clouds flew up into the air. Mr and Mrs Gonzalez found themselves picking up handfuls of blossom and hurling it at one another until they were both covered with petals.

The two goats munched eagerly away and found the pink stuff very good to eat, and Hugo the dog decided to try eating the petals too. But he didn't like the taste of the blossom at all and barked at the pink stuff so loudly that everyone collapsed into fits of giggles and laughed until they lay exhausted on the ground.

Spring is here

At almost every house along the street where Samantha
lived, there was a bird-table and a birdbath on the garden
lawn. All through the winter the tables had been loaded with
leftover bread, bacon rinds and birdseed for the hungry
birds to eat. And the birdbaths had been kept full of fresh,
clean water.

'The birds must be very pleased that we look after them so
well,' said Samantha to her mother one day.

'Yes they are,' Samantha's mummy said. 'And they'll
thank us in the spring. You'll see.'

'You will tell me when the birds come to thank us, won't
you Mummy?' said Samantha.

'Yes Sam, I promise I will tell you,' laughed Mummy.

Samantha waited eagerly for spring. She was longing to
know what would happen. One morning Mummy crept into
her room very, very early. Gently she shook her awake.

'Put your dressing gown and slippers on and come to the
window,' she whispered.

Opening it, they heard hundreds of birds all singing at the
same time.

'It's beautiful Mummy,' said Samantha.

'It's called the early morning chorus,' Mummy explained.
'It means that spring is here at last.'

The polar bear

Benedict the polar bear was feeling very happy. 'The sun is out. Spring is starting,' he said as he jumped across the ice floes on the river.

But no sooner had he said that when – whoooosh, whoooosh, wooooo, wooooo – a huge gale started to blow. It blew a blizzard of freezing rain everywhere, and it was so strong that it blew rocks and stones about. It blew everything – even Benedict himself!

'I am very cross about this,' said Benedict. 'How can I go hunting for food when the wind blows so hard? How can I see to catch fish with snow blowing in my eyes?'

Then – a very funny thing happened. Lots of empty boxes appeared, blown along by the gale.

'It's raining boxes,' said Benedict, 'and those boxes smell of food. I will go on a hunt to find out where they came from.'

So when the gale stopped Benedict set off. He followed the trail of boxes until he came to an Eskimo village. And behind the village shop, lying in the snow, were lots and lots of broken eggs. They must have fallen out of the boxes.

'What a lovely spring dinner,' said Benedict as he licked up all the eggs in the spring sunshine.

'What a huge, hungry polar bear!' said all the children watching him through their windows.

When Benedict had finished all the eggs he said, 'Eggs are very nice for a change, but fish are much nicer!' And he went back to the river.

Maggie's budgerigar

'You are the nicest budgerigar in all the world,' said Maggie to her pet budgie Bobby as she played a game with him.

Bobby was perched on top of the table and he was playing ping-pong. Maggie rolled a ping-pong ball towards him, and Bobby pushed it back to her with his beak.

Just then, Maggie's mummy came in. 'How would you like to go on holiday to Australia?' Mummy asked Maggie.

'Oh yes please Mum,' said Maggie. 'Will we go in an aeroplane?'

'Yes,' said Mum, 'and we'll be able to visit Aunty Gwen and Uncle Mike and all your cousins. It will be really exciting.'

Then Maggie said, 'Will Bobby be able to come as well?'

'I'm afraid Bobby can't possibly come with us,' said Mum. Then she had an idea: 'I know – we can ask Gran to look after him until we get back again. How's that?'

Maggie nodded, but secretly she was very sad at having to leave Bobby at home with Gran. And all the way to Australia on the aeroplane she kept thinking about him. 'I hope I don't forget what he looks like,' she said to Mum. 'And I hope Gran will play ping-pong with him and let him fly about.'

Even when they got off the aeroplane and saw the lovely sandy beaches and sparkling sea Maggie still felt a bit sad. But when they got to the farm where her Aunty Gwen and Uncle Mike lived she got a very big surprise. For in all the trees around the farm there seemed to be lots and lots of green birds that looked just the same as Bobby.

'They *are* budgerigars,' said Aunty Gwen. 'Budgerigars live in the trees in Australia, just like sparrows do where you live.'

Then Maggie told them all about her budgerigar called
Bobby who could play ping-pong. And she wasn't lonely any
longer because it was springtime and there were so many
budgerigars to see.

When they got home from their Australian holiday
Maggie told Bobby why she hadn't been lonely. 'But those
budgerigars weren't as clever as you,' she said. 'They
couldn't play ping-pong!'

Georgie's daffodils

One very cold day when there were no leaves on the trees and it was raining and miserable, Georgie's mum went to the shops and bought some plastic daffodils. They were bright yellow, and she let Georgie put them in a big vase.

'Are plastic flowers *real* flowers, Mum?' asked Georgie.

'No,' said his mum. 'They are toy flowers. They don't grow and they don't need water like real flowers, but they look nice and cheerful. Some people can't tell the difference between plastic flowers and real flowers!'

Georgie liked the plastic daffodils. They lasted for ever and ever. Then one day in spring, his mum said, 'I wish we had some proper daffodils. Real daffodils are a sign of spring.'

So the next time they were near a flower shop and Georgie was on his own with his dad he whispered, 'Dad – is it nearly spring?'

'Yes,' said his dad.

'Can I buy Mum some real daffodils, then?' asked Georgie.

'Yes,' said his dad smiling.

When Georgie and his dad got home, Mum was out. So

Georgie took the plastic daffodils out of the vase. Then he filled the vase with water and put the real daffodils in. They looked beautiful! He took the plastic ones outside and stuck them in the earth near the front door: one, two, three, four, five, six plastic daffodils in the garden. He had just got back indoors when Mum came in with Auntie Posy.

'What beautiful daffodils,' said Auntie Posy looking at Mum's vase of flowers. 'The first sign of spring. I noticed you had some outside your front door, too.'

Then Mum said, 'I didn't know the ones in the garden were ready yet, but if they are out Georgie will pick some for you. I'm afraid the ones in that vase are only plastic!'

'Plastic ones?' said Auntie Posy in amazement. 'They look just like real ones!'

Then Georgie and his dad began to laugh. 'The garden ones are plastic,' Georgie said. 'Go and look at the daffodils in the vase again, Mum.'

'They're real ones!' gasped Mum. 'Beautiful fresh spring daffodils.'

And when they had tea she put them right in the middle of the table – and Georgie felt very proud.

The seed

The seed lay quietly in the hard ground. 'It's too cold to grow,' it said sadly.

But when the days grew longer and the sun grew stronger, the seed began to stir in the warm earth. 'I've started growing,' cried the seed joyfully, and it burst open and sent down a little root into the soil. Through the root it sucked up food and water.

Then it pushed a shoot upwards through the earth. 'I want to climb up and see the sky,' it said, growing faster.

Soon the seed shot out of the ground. It uncurled two leaves that turned green in the sunlight. After that there was no stopping the seed. It raced upwards growing more and more leaves.

One day, the seed decided to grow a flower with five bright yellow petals. Can you guess what it had grown into?

It had grown into a buttercup.

And the buttercup was so proud of its golden flower that it decided to grow lots more and the flowers bloomed prettily in the corner of the field all summer long.

Spring cleaning

One day, at the end of the winter, Mother said, 'I think we will start spring cleaning the house today. Will you help me, Anthony?'

'Ooh, yes,' said Anthony.

They started upstairs. Mother took down the curtains and washed them and hung them on the clothes line outside. Anthony helped to take all the blankets and sheets and pillowcases off the beds so that they could be washed as well.

While Mother cleaned the windows Anthony tidied his toy drawer. Then Mother said, 'If I pull this cupboard forward just slightly, could you squeeze in behind it and dust away any cobwebs, please?'

She gave Anthony a big yellow duster.

It was a heavy cupboard – too heavy to move very far but Mother managed to make a little space for Anthony to get round the back.

'Ooh, there *are* some cobwebs,' he told his mother and then he saw something else, something shining on the floor. He bent down to see what it was.

'I've found your brooch, Mummy,' he called. 'The one you thought you'd lost.'

'Well, fancy that!' said Mother. 'I've looked everywhere for it. What a good thing I had you to help me spring clean or I might never have found it.'

33

Valentina's ribbon

Valentina, á Russian girl with rosy cheeks, Shamroo, an Indian boy with big dark eyes, and Chiyo, a Japanese boy with a round, jolly face, all lived in a children's home.

It was a very happy place and the children often had parties. In the spring every year they had a party with lots of chocolate Easter eggs to eat.

'I wish I had something special to wear for the spring party,' said Valentina to Shamroo and Chiyo when she saw them all dressed up.

Shamroo had a new blue shirt and Chiyo wore his best leather sandals.

Then she remembered her special treasure. It was a red ribbon she kept in a little box. 'I'll wear my ribbon,' she said, and she tied the ribbon to her long shining hair. But her hair was so shiny and smooth that the ribbon slipped off as soon as the party started.

'Don't be sad. We'll find it for you,' said all the other children. And they ran off into the garden to hunt for it.

'Even Pod the puppy is trying to find the ribbon,' laughed Chiyo as Pod sniffed about in the grass wagging his tail.

'Found it!' shouted Shamroo. 'It was near the gate.' And Shamroo had found the ribbon, but oh dear, it was all creased and crumpled now.

'It's not a party ribbon any longer,' said Valentina sadly as she put it in her pocket.

But Valentina had a nice surprise because at the end of the party when everyone was given a chocolate Easter egg – guess what Valentina's egg had tied around it! A beautiful new piece of bright red ribbon.

Then Valentina had a good idea and she said to Pod the puppy, 'Because you tried to find my ribbon for me – I'm going to give *you* a present too.' And she put the old ribbon round Pod's neck. 'And now everyone is ready for springtime,' she said.

Baby animals

Graham went to stay with his auntie on her farm for his spring holidays. Living in the city, he had never stayed on a farm before. 'What will it be like?' he thought as he arrived there.

When he saw how big the bull was, he was scared, and when he saw how fierce the large cockerel was, he backed away, and when the geese hissed at him he ran and hid under the kitchen table.

'You'll soon get used to all the animals, Graham,' said his auntie laughing.

'No I won't,' insisted Graham. 'They are all either too big or too fierce.'

'Then tomorrow morning, if you get up early, you can help me feed all the little animals,' said Auntie. Graham was puzzled – he hadn't seen any 'little' animals.

The following morning, Graham got a surprise. First his auntie took him into a special cowshed. 'Don't forget that it is spring. Spring is when all the animals are having their babies,' she said.

'Oh how sweet,' said Graham as he saw the tiny calf feeding from its mother. 'I think I like cows after all.'

Then they went into a heated place where there were hundreds of tiny fluffy chicks. Graham was allowed to hold one in his hands. It was soft and yellow. 'I think I like chickens after all,' Graham decided.

Next they fed the ducks and geese on the pond. Graham saw some baby goslings and ducklings swimming along with their mothers. 'I like geese as well now,' said Graham as he threw them some small crumbs of bread.

'Auntie, I like being on a farm,' said Graham at the end of his visit. 'May I come again next spring? I'm not so frightened of the big animals any more either.'

'Yes of course you can, and next year you can even help me to feed the bull,' laughed his auntie.

Mr Crocodile

Josie's dad looked after a river full of crocodiles in Africa. One day when Josie and her dad were in a boat on the river, her dad said, 'We must keep away from the crocodiles. Mr Crocodile is extra fierce today.'

Suddenly they saw Mr Crocodile's snout pop up from the water. It was very long with lots of sharp pointed teeth shining in his huge open jaws.

'He is guarding the river,' said Josie's dad. 'He will bite anything that goes near him with his huge jaws.'

'Why is he extra fierce today, Dad?' asked Josie.

'He has a secret,' said Dad smiling. 'Can you see that long grass over there? Well, there is a nest full of crocodile eggs hidden behind it. And Mrs Crocodile is there too.'

'How many eggs will there be?' asked Josie.

'Guess,' said Dad.

'Six?' said Josie.

'More than that,' said Dad.

'Sixteen?' said Josie.

'Try again,' said Dad. 'There will be a lot more than that.'

'Forty!' said Josie laughing.

'Right,' said Dad. 'There will be about forty eggs in the nest.'

And a few weeks later forty sharp little crocodile snouts broke through the egg shells and forty baby crocodile heads popped out.

'They all look like Mr Crocodile,' laughed Josie. 'So *that* was his secret.'

Rabbits!

'Don't our cabbage seedlings look nice?' said Emily to her brother Nicholas. 'Soon they'll grow into fresh green cabbages. Won't Daddy be pleased!'

When Daddy got home from work at teatime they took him into the garden to show him the two neat rows of little green leaves.

But Daddy looked very puzzled. 'Baby cabbages?' he said. 'I can only see grass and a few weeds.'

Emily said to Nicholas, 'Something ate those baby cabbages and I'll bet it was rabbits!'

So the next morning they both got up extra early to see.

'Just look through this window,' gasped Emily. 'There are lots of baby rabbits nibbling everything – with two big rabbits on guard.'

'We must chase them away,' said Nicholas, and they both dashed outside.

When they told Dad who had eaten the cabbages, he got some green garden netting to spread over the next lot of seedlings.

Tibs the cat helped guard the seedlings too. She sat on the wall and kept a look out for baby rabbits.

The sleepy tortoise

Bill the zoo keeper was very worried. His giant tortoise Stanley was *still* asleep!

'I hope he wakes up soon,' said Bill to all the children, one spring day. 'It will be his birthday soon. I hope he won't sleep for ever and ever. He's very old is Stanley. Very, very big and very, very old. He's older than all you children. He's older than me. And he's older than my grandad. He'll be a hundred years old on his next birthday – if he wakes up.' And Bill looked more worried than ever.

Stanley liked living at the zoo because people were very kind to him and sometimes gave him treats – like strawberries and yellow dandelion flowers to eat. But every autumn when the weather got colder, he would go into the corner of his pen and burrow into the soil and go fast asleep until the warm spring weather came back again. But this year Stanley stayed asleep even when the warm spring weather came.

One day, Bill said sadly to the children, 'It will be Stanley's birthday on Saturday – but I'm afraid he won't be awake in time.'

Then suddenly one of the children shouted, 'Stanley's waking up!' And slowly, very slowly, the earth in the corner of the pen began to move. And slowly, very slowly, Stanley's shell appeared. And slowly, very slowly, his head came out from the shell and he opened his eyes.

'He must have heard us!' gasped Bill. 'He doesn't want to miss his party after all.'

Bill was so delighted that he rushed away and came back with a big cabbage for Stanley to eat and quickly, very quickly, Stanley ripped off the green spring leaves with his huge jaws and crunched them up.

'He's woken up properly at last!' said everyone. And they were so pleased, they all came to Stanley's one hundredth birthday party and brought their own little pet tortoises too.

The bicycle ride

One day, Dad came home from work with a strange bicycle. 'It's a tandem,' he said. 'It's a bicycle made for two.'

'But we need a bicycle made for five, Dad,' said Poppy, 'because there's me and Mum and Toby and Tina as well.'

'There's a sidecar for Toby and Tina to sit in,' said Mum, 'and there's a seat on the back for you, Poppy.'

So one sunny spring day they all set off on the tandem for a ride into the country.

Dad sat in front and pedalled. Mum sat behind him and pedalled. Poppy sat on the seat behind Mum and the twins sat in the sidecar. The twins and Poppy waved to everyone they passed.

After a while they came to a hill and Dad began to puff and pant and he said to Mum, 'Are you pedalling?'

'Yes, I am!' puffed Mum. 'I'm pedalling as hard as I can.'

Then Dad said, 'Stop. We must all get off and push. This hill is too steep.'

'Are we in the countryside yet, Mum?' asked Poppy as she pushed the tandem along.

'Nearly,' gasped Mum. 'It's over the top of this hill.'

When they reached the top of the hill they saw all the countryside spread out – with trees and fields and a river and a farm. Then they all got on the tandem again and whizzed down the hill towards the river.

'No need to pedal, now,' laughed Dad.

But just as they got near the river something happened. The tandem went all wobbly and jolty and the wheels slowed down and went wooomp-plonk, wooomp-plonk, wooomp-plonk and Poppy began to go wooomp-plonk too.

'Off we get,' said Dad. 'We must have hit a sharp stone. The back tyre's burst. We've got a puncture and we can't go on until it's mended.'

Then, just when everyone was struggling away with spanners and bicycle inner tubes and repair kits, a bus stopped by the river and lots of people got out to have a picnic.

'What's up, mate?' said the bus driver to Dad.

'A puncture,' said Dad.

'We'll soon fix it,' said the bus driver as he helped Mum and Dad. And all the passengers shared their big picnic with Mum, Dad, Poppy and the twins.

The merry moles

One spring day a sad thing happened to Miriam. She was covered in spots and had to stay in bed.

'Cheer up,' said Mum, 'I'll read you a story about three merry moles who made magic castles.'

'Once upon a time,' said Mum, 'there were three merry little moles and they all had pointed noses, thick dark fur coats, and the most amazing creamy pink paws. And because they had such big paws they all dug enormous molehills to live in.

'But one day it rained so much that those merry moles were flooded out and their molehills were completely spoilt.

'"We must find new lands for our castles," said the first mole. "But where can we go? Lots of people don't like our molehills."

'"Let's go to Fairyland, then," said the second mole. And so they did . . .'

'Miriam's gone to Fairyland too. She's fast asleep,' smiled Mum tip-toeing away.

When Miriam woke next morning, she had two nice surprises – her spots had gone and out in the garden something was happening. Molehills were growing up out of the ground before her very eyes.

'Magic molehills!' laughed Miriam. 'The moles have come here instead of Fairyland after all!'

Avatak

Avatak's father took the kayak down from the rack where he kept it all through the long dark winter.

'This needs mending before we go to summer camp,' he said, looking at the holes in the boat's sealskin sides.

So Avatak's mother began to stitch new sealskins for the kayak.

Avatak sat watching. Behind their hut he could see his friends sliding down the hillside on the hard-packed snow. Each child sat on a piece of sealskin or polar bear skin.

Avatak loved sliding, but he had nothing to sit on. He looked around inside the hut.

Hanging on the wall was the foxtail his mother used for wrapping round sore throats. By the lamp lay his brother's best sealskin mittens. On the bed were his father's new polar bear skin trousers.

He sighed. There was nothing here he could use to slide down the hill. Sadly he went outside again.

'What's the matter, Avatak?' asked his mother.

'All my friends are sliding this morning, but I can't find anything to sit on,' he said.

'I've finished mending the kayak,' replied his mother, 'and I think there's a piece of sealskin left over for you.'

Avatak was delighted, and he raced up the hill for his first slide of the summer.

Wind and sun

The wind woke up in a temper, feeling cross. It blew the clouds into black grumpy shapes, made the river grey and angry, and slammed doors and windows. No one liked the wind that day.

'You've rattled my lid!' grumbled the dustbin.

'You've taken off our leaves,' sighed the trees.

'You've blown out my candles,' said the birthday cake.

'You've taken my kite,' cried the little boy.

'You've untied my hair ribbons,' scowled the little girl.

'You've torn my newspaper,' shouted Dad.

'You've blown my washing off the line,' groaned Mum.

'You've ruffled my fur,' miaowed the cat.

'You've knocked my hat off,' scolded the little old lady.

And all the people went into their houses and shut the doors.

The wind didn't care. It whirled off and blew at a few more clouds. But it blew so hard that it blew them right away. And out came the sun! The wind stopped blowing in surprise.

When they saw the sun, all the people came out of their houses again, to enjoy feeling the warm summer sunshine and see the blue sky. The sun was pleased to be liked, and it grew hotter and hotter. But it grew so hot that all the people went indoors again.

'Let's be friends,' said the sun to the wind. 'Let's work together to make people happy.'

So they did. The sunny windows gleamed, and the big river sparkled again. There was a little patch of warmth for the cat to sit in, and the trees spread out their leaves.

The little old lady put on her straw hat again, and even the dustbin stopped rattling and settled down quietly.

Mum's washing dried, and Dad sat in a deckchair to read his newspaper.

The wind tugged gently at the little boy's kite, and it soared up into the blue sky.

The little girl found her hair ribbons, caught safely on a rosebush, and wore them to a party.

At the party the cake's candles were lit again, and this time they stayed alight.

'It's been a lovely day, after all,' said the people, and the sun and the wind were pleased.

The cheese barge

Pieter and Marika jumped down into the barge. For the next three weeks they would be cruising along the canals of north Holland in a barge called *The Black Tulip*.

Pieter and Marika liked travelling by barge. They could see everything for miles around and other barges passed them loaded with milk churns, or red and yellow flowers for the flower market.

Early one Friday morning Pieter and Marika were woken by their father starting the engine. 'We're going to the cheese market at Alkmaar,' he said.

The barge chugged off up the canal. Pieter and Marika sat on the cabin roof. Most of the barges they saw today were loaded with red and yellow cheeses shaped like footballs.

'I should like to run a cheese barge when I grow up,' said Pieter.

'I hope we get there soon,' said Marika. She liked cheese so much Father often called her Mouse instead of Marika.

Suddenly, round a bend in the canal, they came upon a barge that had stopped.

'We're going to crash,' yelled Pieter, but Father steered away just in time.

'Do you need any help?' Father called.

'We've got engine trouble,' said one of the men in the barge, 'and these cheeses have to go to the market today.'

Father got out on to the bank and talked to them for a few minutes. Then he came back with the younger bargeman.

'Now's your chance, Pieter,' he said. 'They're going to use our barge to carry the cheeses to market.'

The man on the cheese barge began to unload by throwing the cheeses over the side into *The Black Tulip*. The young bargeman caught them neatly and stacked them wherever he could find a space. Soon there were cheeses everywhere.

As they tied up at Alkmaar with the other cheese barges, Pieter and Marika felt very proud. Their barge looked just like the real thing.

Two porters wearing straw hats with red ribbons trotted up with their red barrow. Father and the bargeman started throwing the cheeses to the porters, who loaded the barrows and trotted back to the market without dropping one.

'I've changed my mind,' said Pieter. 'I think I'll be a porter when I grow up and have a red barrow and red ribbons on my hat.'

'As long as you always remember to bring some cheese home for me,' said Marika.

The cowboy hat

Nicky woke up early on his birthday. It was summer, warm and sunny, and on his bed he could see one of his presents – a smart cowboy hat.

Nicky put it on and leaned back happily against the pillows. He fired an imaginary gun into the air.

'Ouch!' said a cross, prickly voice. Nicky found that he was looking at an enormous cactus.

'Here's a horse for you to ride,' said the cactus.

'But I don't know how to ride a horse,' said Nicky.

'Please yourself,' said the cactus, and vanished. Nicky straightened his hat and clambered on to the horse – and he was at a rodeo show! It was hot and dusty with crowds of people there. They cheered him as his horse galloped about, and he brandished his pistol and whirled his lasso.

Suddenly the horse bolted. Nicky hung on tightly, and the sound of cheering followed him.

'Hurrah! He's woken up! Happy birthday!' Nicky's brothers were shouting.

'I've been at a rodeo show. It was very hot,' said Nicky.

'No wonder you're hot,' said his mother. 'You're wearing your hat in bed. Wake up – you're going to have an exciting day.'

'I've had an exciting day already,' said Nicky.

The weather house

A smart, new weather house stood on the windowsill in Mrs Brown's cottage.

On sunny days, out came the weather lady. Her job was to tell Mrs Brown when the weather was going to be sunny.

On wet days, the weather man came outside with his umbrella to tell Mrs Brown that it was going to rain.

Then, one morning, the weather man and the weather lady had a surprise. The weather wasn't sunny and it wasn't wet. There was no sun – nor was there any rain. It was just a dull day.

The weather lady wasn't sure what to do. Then she decided to stay indoors. The weather man made up his mind to stay indoors, too.

Inside the weather house, the weather man and the weather lady met for the first time.

'Let's have lunch together, and a cosy chat,' said the weather man.

They had a marvellous time, and agreed to meet on every dull day.

'I like sunny days, and you like wet days,' said the weather lady, 'but now we both like dull days too.'

Snowfoot's calf

Every year Inger and her family left their home in the high mountains of Norway and drove their reindeer herd across the snow to the coast for the summer. There the reindeer ate the rich green grass and grew fat ready for the winter.

Inger's father liked the whole family to make the journey together, as the Lapps did in the old days. So Inger and her grandmother sat in an old-fashioned sledge pulled by her father's snow-scooter.

Inger's grandmother often told her stories of the journeys in the old days. Then all the sledges were pulled by reindeer and the journey took much longer.

Soon the herd would reach the coast. They were late this year because one of the snow-scooters had skidded and bumped into a tree. It had taken Inger's father three days to mend it. The snow was becoming softer as the weather grew warmer, and the snow-scooters did not go so fast.

'I hope we have no more hold-ups,' said Inger's father. 'I don't want any reindeer calves born on the way. They can't keep up with the herd.'

'But we couldn't leave a calf behind,' said Inger.

'In the old days, that's what happened,' said her grandmother.

Next morning Inger's father went out early to look at the herd. When he came back, he looked worried.

'Inger,' he said, 'your reindeer, Snowfoot, had a calf in the night. It is very, very small.'

Inger had been given Snowfoot on her last birthday, and she loved the gentle reindeer with her soft, brown hair and dark eyes.

'How many more days to the coast, Father?' she asked.

'Perhaps two, perhaps three,' he said.

'Let me go and see the calf,' said Inger.

The new calf lay next to Snowfoot. He was very, very small. 'But he's lovely,' said Inger. 'I shall call him Snowball.'

Her grandmother came up to look. 'He is a fine calf,' she said, 'even if he is small. He'll soon be big enough to keep up with the rest of the herd. Till then he can ride on the sledge with Inger and me.'

'There won't be much room for three of you,' said Inger's father.

'I don't mind,' said Inger, 'and he'll be safe from the wild animals with us.'

So Inger and her grandmother and Snowball were all riding happily together in the sledge, as her father drove the snow-scooter down the track to the summer camp.

The little pond

Goldie and Sammy were two beautiful goldfish, who lived in a big pond. They were very happy until, one day, Goldie found herself being caught in a fishing net. How cross she was when she was tipped into a bucket of water. Sammy was tipped in beside her. The bucket was picked up and taken to another, smaller pond in the same garden, and emptied into it.

'I don't like it here!' gurgled Sammy. 'There isn't enough room. We'll have to take turns at swimming. And it is too hot because there are no rocks to hide behind, and no pretty water lilies or bulrushes.'

Goldie didn't like the little pond either. She and Sammy stayed there for several hours, feeling very sorry for themselves.

Then, just when they were thinking they would never see their own, lovely pond again – the fishing net plopped into the water beside them. Someone swirled the net around until Sammy and Goldie were caught inside it.

'Back into that bucket again, I suppose!' spluttered Sammy.

He was right, but he and Goldie did not stay in the bucket for long – just long enough to be carried back to their own, dear pond.

They almost leapt from the bucket when they saw their pond again. They were sure it was their own pond, but it looked different. The green weed had been taken out, and the rocks tidied. Some of the water-grasses had been cut down, and the water looked clear and clean.

'Some kind person has cleaned and tidied our pond,' gurgled Sammy. And the two fish swam round and round happily in their nice clean pond.

The butterfly bush

'We're having tea with Aunt Pat today, Tim,' said Mother. 'She has a butterfly bush in her garden.'

Tim was puzzled. Butterflies don't grow on bushes. Butterflies come from caterpillars. Everyone knows that.

During tea Tim kept looking out of the window, but he couldn't see a butterfly bush anywhere.

'Tim can't wait to see your butterfly bush,' said Mother.

So after tea Aunt Pat took him up to the top of the garden. 'There it is,' she said. 'That big bush with the clusters of tiny purple flowers.'

The bush looked like a magic picture – brightly coloured butterflies dancing in and out of the long branches, settling on the flowers, opening and closing their wings in the sunshine.

'I know why it's called a butterfly bush now,' said Tim. 'Butterflies don't grow on it, but they like visiting it.'

When it was time to go home Tim said, 'I wish we had a butterfly bush in our garden.'

'Shall we plant one in our garden?' said Mother.

'Yes please,' said Tim. 'My very own butterfly bush.'

Under the sea

Under the sea no one liked Garry Crab. 'You're crabby!' said the starfish. 'You're always cross and grumpy.'

Poor Garry Crab!

'Cheer up!' said Jerry Jellyfish. 'You're not the only one who isn't liked. No one likes me either.'

The starfish had to agree. 'You're often bad-tempered,' the starfish told Jerry Jellyfish. 'And when you are in one of your bad tempers – you sting. No one likes being stung.'

Garry Crab looked thoughtful. 'I don't mind being stung,' he said. 'You see, I don't feel stings. My hard shell protects me. Perhaps you and I should be friends, Jerry. We'll live together in that empty cave.'

Jerry Jellyfish looked a little less cross than usual, and the two new friends went to the cave straightaway to set up home together.

Garry Crab was pleased to have a new friend who liked him. In fact, he was so pleased that he wasn't crabby or cross or grumpy any more.

Jerry Jellyfish was so pleased to have a new friend that he forgot all about being bad-tempered. Because he wasn't bad-tempered, he didn't sting any more.

Soon all the underwater folk liked Garry and Jerry – even the starfish!

Bigboots the giant

No one liked Bigboots the giant. He was always boasting
and showing off. He picked up houses and put them down
in different places. He blew all the water out of the duck-
pond. He uprooted trees and squashed people's gardens.

The king heard about this naughty giant and he decided
to teach him a lesson. He summoned Bigboots to the palace.

Bigboots was a bit scared because, deep down, he knew he
had been very naughty. But, to his surprise, the king didn't
scold him. Instead he asked Bigboots to help him.

'My gardener – Tinytoes the elf – is finding it too difficult
to look after all the palace gardens on his own,' the king said.
'So I thought you might like to help him. You can look
after the gardens on the west side of the palace, and Tinytoes

will look after the gardens on the east side.'

Now it was a great honour to be asked to help with the palace gardens. They were famous all over the kingdom.

Bigboots felt sure that he would be a marvellous gardener and he looked at Tinytoes scornfully. 'I shall grow wonderful flowers,' he said boastfully. 'I'm surprised that a tiny elf can do anything at all! I shall be a much better gardener than him.'

The king just smiled to himself and said nothing.

Bigboots started work. He was very good at digging the ground. He was very good at pulling up weeds. He was even quite good at mowing the grass. But he was no good at all at planting seeds, or looking after little tiny plants. His fingers were so big he couldn't hold the seeds! And his feet were so big he trod on all the baby plants!

In the winter Bigboots laughed at Tinytoes trying to clear up the gardens and dig the earth. But when summer came Tinytoes laughed because he had lots and lots of beautiful flowers and Bigboots had none.

When the king came to inspect the gardens one hot summer's day Bigboots hung his head. 'Well,' said the king, 'I hope you have learnt your lesson, Bigboots. You may be good at some things but you are not good at everything. No one is good at everything. Now if you both work together the gardens will be better than ever!'

The cuckoo clock

Once upon a time there was a cuckoo who lived in a clock which belonged to a little girl called Trudi. Trudi lived in a pretty little chalet in Switzerland. She was very fond of her clock. She loved to see the funny cuckoo pop out of the clock every hour, calling, 'Cuckoo!' to tell her the time.

One summer's day the cuckoo heard the birds singing. He thought he would like to fly about too, and have an adventure. So, when he popped out of his clock to announce it was morning, he flew right out of the chalet, singing, 'In July away I fly!'

First of all the cuckoo flew over blue lakes and green mountain slopes to a town. He perched on the Town Hall clock at ten o'clock and called, 'Cuckoo, cuckoo, cuckoo, cuckoo, cuckoo, cuckoo, cuckoo, cuckoo, cuckoo, cuckoo!'

The Mayor was quite upset and dropped all his important papers. 'Go away, you silly bird,' he said crossly.

The cuckoo flew about the town and saw a friendly looking weathercock sitting on top of a church. 'Cuckoo, cuckoo, cuckoo, cuckoo, cuckoo, cuckoo, cuckoo, cuckoo, cuckoo, cuckoo, cuckoo, cuckoo!' shouted the cuckoo. 'It's noon!'

But the weathercock wasn't so friendly after all. The wind changed and he turned his back without speaking.

So off went the cuckoo again, right out of the town and into the meadows. But the cuckoo couldn't find anyone who wanted to know the time. He told a cow that it was two o'clock, but she didn't care. He told a horse that it was four o'clock but he wasn't interested.

The cuckoo decided to go home to his clock. And home he flew, calling, 'Cuckoo, cuckoo, cuckoo, cuckoo, cuckoo! Time for tea!'

Trudi was delighted to see him again. 'Was it fun having an adventure?' she asked.

'No,' said the cuckoo. 'Nobody really wanted to know what the time was. Was it fun without me?'

'No,' said Trudi. 'I didn't know when it was time for lunch. You really were a silly bird to fly away.'

Mingo the monkey

The sun blazed down on the jungle. All the animals were sleeping under the trees, except Mingo the monkey who swung along the branches, scaring the birds and annoying the other animals. He dropped out of the trees on top of the tiger, uncoiled the snake, and pulled the lion's tail.

The animals got cross with him, so he went and sat down for a rest, on a rock by the edge of the cool river.

But the rock moved, and started to float away! 'Hey!' squealed Mingo. 'Whatever's happening?'

The rock slowly winked an eye. It was the crocodile! 'I'm taking you for a ride,' smiled the crocodile, swimming a little faster.

Mingo was rather scared. The water rushed past and the crocodile smiled and all his great white crocodile teeth gleamed in the sun.

Then suddenly, the crocodile opened his huge mouth, and, 'Snap!' He shut his mouth again, tossing Mingo into the air.

Mingo fell into the water and when he reached the bank all wet and dripping, he found all the animals sitting there laughing at him.

'That serves you right for teasing us when it is so hot,' they said.

'Well,' said Mingo, 'at least I am nice and cool now!'

At the market

Jason and his family were camping in the countryside. One sunny morning they went to the market in a nearby village, with Dandy their dog.

The market was very interesting. There were stalls with fruit and vegetables, stalls with eggs and cheese, stalls with fish, and stalls with brown, crusty bread.

There were a lot of people at the market but they were too busy and excited to notice a black cat creeping round the side of the fish stall. But Jason saw it – just as it jumped right up to steal the fish.

'Puss! Get down!' cried Jason, but the cat didn't seem to hear. Then Dandy saw it. 'Woof! Woof!' he barked, and pulled his lead out of Jason's hand. Dandy chased the cat, hitting the stalls as he ran. The cat fled, but one of the stalls collapsed. Fruit rolled everywhere, and all the people waved their arms about and shrieked.

Dandy trotted back, trying to look ashamed. But the market people forgave him – because he was trying to save the fish. And Jason got a reward for spotting the thief – a big juicy orange!

Daniel the dragon

One very sunny day, Daniel the dragon saw some children standing in a long line beside a van.

'Come and join us, Daniel,' they called. 'We're waiting to be served by the ice-cream man.'

'What *is* ice-cream?' Daniel asked.

'It's cold, and sweet and lovely,' said the children. 'You'll like it.'

When Daniel's turn came to be served, he chose a pink ice-cream cornet. A boy called Alexander held the cornet up high, and Daniel stretched down his long neck and licked at the pink ice-cream. 'Delicious!' he said.

'While we eat our ices, Daniel, will you do your best trick for us?' asked Alexander. 'Will you breath smoke rings?'

Now, everyone knows that dragons can breathe smoke and flames, but what Daniel didn't know was that the cold ice-cream had put out his dragon fire! When Daniel tried to breathe smoke, he couldn't even make one tiny ring!

The children were disappointed. 'Perhaps dragons shouldn't eat ice-cream,' said Alexander.

'Oh how sad!' sighed Daniel. 'The ice-cream was so cool and lovely that I wanted to have one on every summer day.'

Daniel looked so upset that the ice-cream man left his
van for a while and came to talk to the dragon.

'I have an idea, Daniel,' he said. 'I'll make you some
special ice-creams, and I'll flavour them with hot, spicy
things like mustard, and pepper and ginger. Hot spicy
things like that will keep your fire going, I'm sure.'

The next day, the ice-cream man returned, and Daniel
chose three of his special ices. One was mustard flavoured,
one ginger and one pepper.

'How horrid!' said Alexander.

He held up the cornets, and Daniel licked off the three
ice-creams. 'They're delicious,' he said. 'They are lovely
and cold, and yet they taste hot. They make me feel cool,
but my tummy feels nice and fiery.'

When Daniel had finished his special ice-creams, he blew
the best smoke rings that he had ever blown.

The circus parade

'I can't sleep, Sergei,' complained Natasha. 'It's too light.'

Her brother smiled. 'It's always like this in Leningrad in the summer. That's why they call it the White Nights, because it doesn't get really dark.'

Natasha leaned out of the window. 'People are still walking about. It's like daytime. I wish we could go out.'

'What about Grandmother? She wouldn't let us. It's much too late,' Sergei said.

'We could go down the back stairs – just for a few minutes. Grandmother won't hear us. She's talking to her friends,' argued Natasha.

The children dressed quickly and crept downstairs and into the street.

A band came marching down the broad avenue, followed by brightly-painted wagons. There were two lions in the first, a brown bear in the second and three growling tigers in the third.

Behind the wagons trotted six white horses. A girl in gold tights stood on the back of the first horse.

'I wish I could do that,' whispered Natasha.

'You'd fall off,' said Sergei.

Then three large elephants plodded past, followed by a smaller one ridden by a boy with a monkey on his shoulder.

'I'd like to ride the elephant,' said Sergei.

At that moment the monkey leapt into the crowd. The boy stretched out his arm to stop it, and fell off the elephant.

Two clowns ran up to help. 'Are you all right?' they asked.

The boy shook his head. 'My shoulder hurts. I can't ride Nina again tonight . . . and Boris has escaped.'

But Sergei had caught the little monkey by stepping on his lead. 'He didn't get far,' he said, giving the monkey to one of the clowns.

'Thank you,' replied the clown, 'but what are we to do? Ivan can't ride Nina or hold on to this little rascal. Perhaps you and your sister could do it.'

'Of course,' said Sergei and Natasha excitedly.

So the circus parade set off again. Sergei, wearing Ivan's smart red coat, rode Nina and Natasha sat behind him holding Boris.

At last the parade was over. Now everyone knew the circus would open tomorrow.

The children ran home, and arrived just as Grandmother's friends were leaving.

Next day Grandmother took the children to the circus.

When the elephants came on, Ivan waved to Sergei and Natasha as he and Boris rode past on Nina.

'That boy seems to know you,' said Grandmother. 'I wonder why.'

Merry Midsummer!

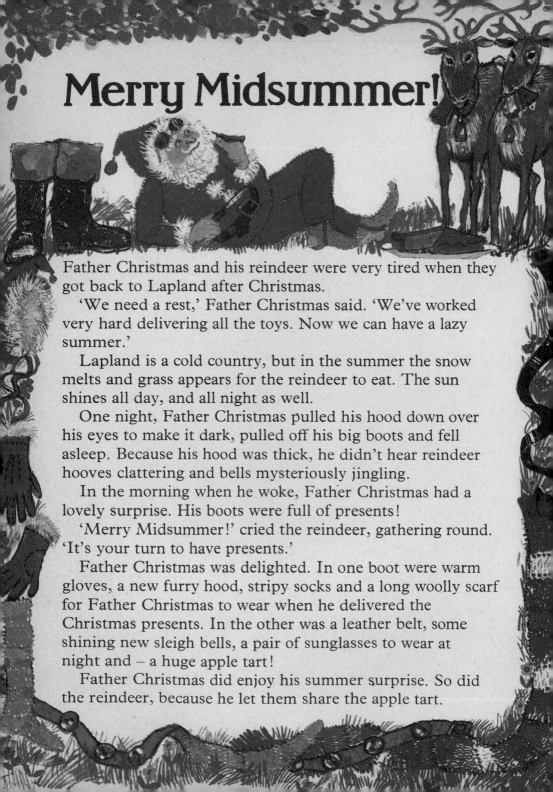

Father Christmas and his reindeer were very tired when they got back to Lapland after Christmas.

'We need a rest,' Father Christmas said. 'We've worked very hard delivering all the toys. Now we can have a lazy summer.'

Lapland is a cold country, but in the summer the snow melts and grass appears for the reindeer to eat. The sun shines all day, and all night as well.

One night, Father Christmas pulled his hood down over his eyes to make it dark, pulled off his big boots and fell asleep. Because his hood was thick, he didn't hear reindeer hooves clattering and bells mysteriously jingling.

In the morning when he woke, Father Christmas had a lovely surprise. His boots were full of presents!

'Merry Midsummer!' cried the reindeer, gathering round. 'It's your turn to have presents.'

Father Christmas was delighted. In one boot were warm gloves, a new furry hood, stripy socks and a long woolly scarf for Father Christmas to wear when he delivered the Christmas presents. In the other was a leather belt, some shining new sleigh bells, a pair of sunglasses to wear at night and – a huge apple tart!

Father Christmas did enjoy his summer surprise. So did the reindeer, because he let them share the apple tart.

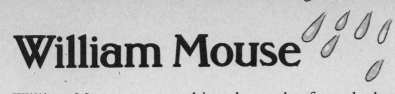

William Mouse

William Mouse was searching the garden for a shady spot to lie in, when he overheard Jonathan talking to his friend. 'I've just been to the seaside,' Jonathan said. 'The sea was lovely and splashy. I paddled in the waves. I wish I could be in the cool sea now.'

'Oh, so do I!' thought William. 'It's so hot today.' William scampered home to Mother Mouse. 'How far away is the sea?' he asked.

'It's a long way away,' said Mother Mouse. 'A little mouse couldn't possibly travel so far.'

William was disappointed. He went back to the garden to try to hear more about the sea but Jonathan and his friend had gone. Instead, Jonathan's father was there watering his vegetables.

'The man is making it rain on his vegetables!' thought William. 'Now he's going indoors and leaving the water running. I'll have some fun.'

William danced about in between the vegetables, and the spray from the sprinkler made him cool. 'Now I'm paddling and splashing just like Jonathan did at the seaside,' squeaked William.

The fruit store

Guy and Claire were spending their August holiday with their parents in a little village on the banks of the great river Loire in France.

One morning they went to market in the next town and bought ten kilos of juicy apples.

Back home Mother laid the apples out in neat rows on the shelves in the spare room. She left a little space between each apple so they wouldn't touch and go bad.

That night Guy woke up feeling hungry. He went to wake Claire. 'I'm going to get an apple,' he whispered. 'Do you want one?'

As the children crept along the corridor, the floorboards creaked loudly.

In the spare room moonlight streamed through the windows and fell on to the apples. They each chose a big rosy apple, and scampered back to bed.

At breakfast Mother said, 'Did you hear a funny noise last night – squeaking and scratching?'

The children looked at each other and tried hard not to giggle.

'I don't mean the noise you two children made, creeping along the corridor to the fruit store,' Mother went on. She smiled as she saw their faces fall. 'I don't mind, but did you hear this other noise?' Guy and Claire shook their heads.

Later that morning Mother came out of the spare room looking cross. 'You may have an apple when you want one,' she said to the children, 'but you must not bite into apples and then put them back.'

'But we didn't,' protested the children.

'Well I don't know how it happened then,' said Mother.

Two nights later Guy and Claire heard scratching and

squeaks coming from the spare room. They jumped out of
bed and ran to the apple store. Claire opened the door
quietly.

There on the shelf, nibbling an apple, crouched a grey,
furry animal with a long bushy tail. 'I'll call Father,' said
Guy.

Father switched on the light and the animal bounded
along the shelf and out of the window squeaking and
snuffling in alarm.

'It's a squirrel,' said Claire.

'I don't think so,' said Father, 'although it's the same size.
I think it was an edible dormouse. They're much bigger
than ordinary dormice. They must live in the woods.'

'And they love apples,' said Mother, holding out three
more nibbled apples. 'And I thought it was you two, when
it was a giant dormouse all the time. We'll close the window
at night from now on, or we'll have no apples left to take
home at the end of the holiday.'

Princess Jasmine

Princess Jasmine lived in Japan. She had a large garden with a lake, cherry trees, and graceful bamboos.

Jasmine was as beautiful and graceful as one of her own bamboos, but she was also vain, spoiled and cross.

One summer day it was her birthday. Her friends Misha, Trisha and little Suki came into the garden where Jasmine sat under the cherry trees.

Her friends bowed low and gave Jasmine birthday gifts –
a kite, paper lanterns, dancing dolls and a picture of a dragon.

But the princess stamped her foot and waved her fan
angrily. 'These presents aren't nearly grand enough for a
princess!' she cried. 'I command you to take them away.'

So Misha, Trisha and little Suki picked up their gifts and
ran away. As little Suki ran away something fell from her
arms to the grass. But Suki didn't notice and ran on.

Suddenly Jasmine felt lonely. 'Come back!' she called,
but there was no reply. She went to see what Suki had
dropped, and saw it was the dragon picture.

To Jasmine's surprise the dragon spoke. 'You're a very
vain, rude, bad-tempered girl,' it scolded. 'In fact, you're
quite horrid. Now, turn me over before I get really angry, so
that I can go back to sleep.'

Jasmine didn't like the look of that dragon, not one little
bit, and she hastily did as she was told. She turned the
picture over, and on the other side was a cross, ugly face.

'What a horrid picture,' said Jasmine. 'Why, it's not a
picture – it's a mirror. And that's me – do I really look like
that?'

'Yes,' laughed her friends, who had been hiding behind
the bamboo bushes. 'Please smile.'

So Jasmine smiled, and found that she felt much happier.
She was sorry for being so cross, and asked her friends to
forgive her, and share her birthday.

She had a wonderful party with her friends who kindly
gave her their presents all over again. They flew the kite,
played with the dolls, and they decorated the garden with
paper lanterns.

It was a lovely party. And now, if Princess Jasmine ever
feels cross again, she picks up the dragon mirror and looks at
her reflection. Then she soon remembers to smile, because
she doesn't want to wake up that dragon again!

The corn dolly

Hannah watched Grandfather thatching his strawstack to keep out the winter rain.

Grandmother came into the stackyard. 'Harvest is nearly over, Hannah, but there's one more job to do.'

Grandmother took Hannah to the cornfield. The prickly stubble crunched beneath their feet. Here and there odd stalks of corn were left standing. Hannah and Grandmother collected them into a bundle.

Back at the farmhouse Grandmother put the cornstalks in water to soften, while she made tea.

'When I was your age, Hannah,' she said, 'the last stalks of corn were made into a corn dolly, and kept in the farmhouse for luck.'

After tea Grandmother started weaving the cornstalks together. She made a long plait which she bent into a horseshoe shape. Then she made a thinner plait with which to hang it on the wall.

'That's not a dolly,' said Hannah, as Grandmother tied a bright red bow to the horseshoe.

Grandmother laughed, 'I always make horseshoes, but you could make a little corn man or even a star.'

She showed Hannah how to make a little corn dolly with the leftover stalks. It was a bit bumpy and lopsided, but Hannah was very pleased with it.

'I'll ask Grandfather to hang it on the stack for luck,' she said.

Emma the elephant

Emma the elephant had no friends. She was only a young elephant, but even so, she was much bigger than all the other jungle children. 'You're clumsy!' they told her. 'You're too big to play with us.'

Then, one day, it was too hot for *any* of the jungle children to play. 'Let's go to the water-hole and have a drink!' said the lion cub.

So the young friends set off to the water-hole together. They saw that Emma was already there. She was filling her long trunk with water, and giving herself a cool shower-bath.

'What fun!' laughed all the jungle children. 'Will you give us shower-baths, too, Emma?'

Emma was delighted that the jungle children seemed to want her, after all. The children queued up, and Emma gave each one a cool shower-bath. Then they queued up all over again! They had cool showers until it got dark.

'Please will you play with us again tomorrow?' they asked. 'We'll meet you at the water-hole early in the morning.'

Of course, happy Emma said, 'Yes!'

Dotty goes swimming

'Would you like to go swimming?' Dad asked Simon and Sarah, one hot day.

'Yes please!' said the children. The swimming pool was in the open air and they both loved going there. Off they hurried to get their swimming things.

Mum and Dotty, their spotted dog, came as well, so that Mum and Dad could go shopping and give Dotty a run in the park, while the children played in the water.

'Here we are,' said Dad, as the car pulled up at the swimming pool.

The children were glad to get out of the car which was hot, although the windows were open to let in the breeze. Soon they were shouting and splashing and having fun in the blue water with the other girls and boys.

In the car, Mum and Dad were sorting out their shopping bags and baskets. They were too busy to notice Dotty, tired of waiting and feeling rather warm, clamber out of one of the open windows.

She ran to the entrance of the swimming pool, squeezed through a gap in the turnstile, and jumped into the cool water with a splash!

The people in the pool thought it was great fun to have a dog swimming with them. Dotty thought it was fun, too. She carried Simon's water wings in her mouth, and pushed

Sarah's ball about with her nose. Everybody clapped.

'Off you go, Dotty, you're very naughty,' scolded Sarah and Simon and chased her out. Dotty was very wet! She left a trail of doggy footprints everywhere as she shook herself and ran back to the car.

By now there was quite a line of traffic. Mum had stopped a policeman, passing in his car, to tell him that they'd lost Dotty. 'She's just vanished, into thin air,' said Mum.

'Water, more like,' said the policeman, as Dotty appeared, wagging her wet tail.

The policeman drove away laughing and Dad put Dotty safely on her lead.

The rest of the traffic moved off slowly. By the time the children had finished their swim and come back to the car, the van at the end of the line had reached the swimming pool. It was the ice-cream van!

'I think we all deserve one,' said Mum, wearily.

Dotty sat up and begged. 'And me?' she barked.

Sofia and the milk

Sofia's mother lifted the heavy bucket up on to the kitchen table, and measured three jugs full of milk into an open pan on the old black stove.

She wore gold earrings which twinkled like little stars when she moved.

When I grow up, thought Sofia, I shall have earrings like gold stars.

'Watch the milk Sofia, while I let the cow out,' called her mother.

The milk was rising up the sides of the pan when Sofia's mother came back. She took it from the stove and put the pan on the stone floor to cool.

Sofia lived on a tiny Greek island, and every summer the Johnson family from England came for their holiday. It was Sofia's job to take them a pan of milk each morning.

Sofia liked her job. When she had delivered the milk she usually played on the beach with Victoria and Katy Johnson.

'The milk is cool now, Sofia,' said her mother feeling the side of the pan. As she turned her head, Sofia saw that one of her mother's earrings was missing.

'Oh dear, I must have lost it when I took the cow out to the field,' said her mother.

Together they began to look for it – on the kitchen floor, in the milking shed, in the yard where the hens scratched, up the path to the field.

At last Sofia's mother said, 'I don't think we'll find it now, and you must hurry with the milk. Mrs Johnson will be waiting.'

Sofia picked up the pan of milk by its two handles and set off down the stony path towards the beach. She saw

Victoria and Katy waving, and started to run.

But she didn't see a large stone lying on the path. Her foot slipped on it, and she fell, spilling the milk which ran away between the stones.

'Are you hurt?' asked Victoria.

'No,' said Sofia rubbing her knees, 'but what about the milk?'

Victoria wasn't listening. She was poking among the stones. 'I saw something shining,' she said.

She moved a big stone, and underneath it lay the little gold star.

'It's Mother's earring!' said Sofia. 'We looked everywhere for it. It must have fallen into the pan.'

Mrs Johnson came out, and Sofia told her what had happened.

'Don't worry about the milk, Sofia,' said Mrs Johnson, 'and I don't think your mother will be cross, do you?'

High tide

Mark and Lucy were playing on the beach. They ran in and out of the waves, which ran up on to the beach like silvery-white horses.

'Let's make a sandcastle,' said Lucy. 'We've just enough time to build it before the tide comes in.'

The castle was beautiful when it was finished, with a moat and turrets. The children stuck two flags into the topmost turret – one red, one blue.

'Let's be king and queen of the castle,' suggested Mark. They put buckets on their heads for crowns and seaweed sashes round their necks, then stood proudly on top of the sandcastle with a spade each for a sceptre.

The tide was coming in fast. An extra large wave swirled round the castle. 'It's giving way!' shouted Mark, and he and Lucy fell into the sand as the castle collapsed.

'Look what I've found,' said Lucy. In her hand was a big, coloured shell.

'Let's listen to the sea,' said Mark, and in turn they put the shell to their ears. They could hear the sea splashing loudly and then a voice said:

> 'Hello, King and Queen,
> Where have you been?
> It's high tide,
> Come for a ride!'

A beautiful seahorse appeared before them and Mark and Lucy climbed on its back and soon they were riding over the waves.

'We really are king and queen,' said Lucy proudly. Their buckets had turned into crowns studded with shells, their

sashes were silk and their spades were gold sceptres.

It was all very exciting. A shoal of little fishes swam by, waving flags patterned with the shape of a silver seahorse.

'Long live the king and queen of the castle!' they cheered, and Mark and Lucy raised their crowns in reply.

The waves grew rougher and it was hard to grip on to the seahorse. They tried to hold on to their crowns but they were slipping down . . . down . . . the tide was going down . . . and Mark and Lucy found themselves back on the beach.

'Well!' said Mark. 'That *was* an adventure. Have you got the shell, Lucy? It must be magic.'

'I must have dropped it,' said Lucy, gathering up the spades, buckets and flags in her search for it among the ruins of their sandcastle. 'I can't see it anywhere. But – surely we only had two flags? Now there are three.'

Lucy was right. There was the red one, the blue one, and one patterned with – a silver seahorse.

Murumbi's question

The ground outside Murumbi's hut was dry and hard. The stream from the waterhole was just a trickle in the dust. Everyone was waiting for the short rains.

'How shall I know when the short rains will start?' Murumbi asked his grandmother.

'You will know,' she said. And that was all she would say.

Murumbi asked the elephant. 'How shall I know when the short rains will start?'

'When the sky is as grey as an elephant's hide, then you will know,' said the elephant.

Murumbi asked the wild dog. 'How shall I know when the short rains will start?'

'When the wind howls across the plain like the howling of a hundred wild dogs, then you will know,' said the wild dog.

Murumbi asked the lion. 'How shall I know when the short rains will start?'

'When the thunder rolls like the roar of a lion and the lightning flashes like a lion's yellow eyes, then you will know,' said the lion.

Next day, Murumbi knew . . .

The sky turned grey as an elephant's hide. The wind howled across the plain like the howling of a hundred wild dogs. The thunder rolled like the roar of a lion. The lightning flashed like a lion's yellow eyes.

And the short rains started.

A shell zoo

One morning Dominic was feeling rather bored. His big brother and sister had just gone back to school after the long summer holidays and he was missing them.

'Why don't you play with some of your toys?' asked Mummy.

'It's no fun without Jill and Patrick,' Dominic said.

His mother thought for a while and then she said, 'I know what you can do. Have you still got all the shells we collected on holiday this year?'

'Yes,' said Dominic, 'but what can I do with them?'

'You can make things,' said Mummy. And while Dominic fetched the shells she hunted through the kitchen drawer and found a tube of glue.

'Look for a big round shell,' she said. Dominic found a big round shell.

'Now look for five little shells,' Mummy said. Dominic hunted through the shells and found five little ones.

Mummy stuck the five little shells to the big round one. 'Look,' she said, 'a tortoise.'

'Can I make one?' asked Dominic.

'Of course,' said Mummy. 'And see if you can think of some other animals to make too.'

By the time Jill and Patrick came home, Dominic had a whole shell zoo to show them.

The wine harvest

Roy and Rachel liked going into the greenhouse in their garden. Inside was a grapevine. It grew all along one side of the greenhouse and, in autumn, there were lots of bunches of green grapes on it.

One Sunday morning when their father was out, Rachel said, 'Let's make some wine, as a surprise!'

'How?' said Roy.

'With the grapes, of course,' said Rachel. 'It's easy – I saw it in a book. You just pick the grapes and then tread on them with your feet, and then put the juice into bottles.'

Roy thought it sounded odd, but he helped Rachel pick some bunches of grapes. They put them in a bucket, and Roy was just going to step into it to tread the grapes, when Rachel shouted, 'Wait! Take your shoes and socks off first!'

They took it in turns to stand in the bucket and stamp up and down on the grapes, which felt all squishy under their bare feet. They poured the juice through a strainer into a jug, and then into an empty lemonade bottle. Rachel made a label saying 'white wine' and stuck it on.

'Whatever's this?' said their father, as they all sat down to lunch.

'It's white wine. We made it!' cried Roy and Rachel together.

'How clever!' said their father. He poured out a small glass, held it up and sniffed it. 'It smells delicious,' he said, raising the glass to his lips.

'We trod it with our own feet!' said Roy proudly.

Their father stopped still, the glass in his hand. 'Really?' he said.

'That's how they do it in some countries, at the wine harvest,' Rachel said.

'I know,' said her father, 'and I've just remembered something else. They always keep the wine for a long time in the bottles, before they drink it. So I'd better pour this back, and we'll put the bottle in the cupboard. I'll look forward to drinking it . . . sometime.'

Roy and Rachel were a bit disappointed, but they cheered up when their father brought out a bottle of lemonade and poured some out for them. 'You'll like this,' he said. 'It's fresh from this year's lemonade harvest!'

Sitting on the floor

Eliza and Darren liked sitting on the floor. They sat on the floor to drink their milk in the morning and they sat on the floor to watch television in the evening. And they always played with their toys on the floor.

Their mother laughed at them. 'We don't need chairs in this house,' she said. 'You two are always sitting on the floor.'

'It's more comfortable sitting on the floor,' said Eliza.

'Yes,' said Darren, 'and there's more room to play with our toys.'

'Well as long as you two are happy I don't mind,' said Mummy.

Then one day Mummy came in to the sitting room to find both the children sitting quietly on the settee and looking bored. 'What's the matter with you two?' she asked.

'We were making a jigsaw,' said Eliza.

'Yes,' said Darren, 'we were making a jigsaw over there on the floor by the French windows.'

'But,' said Eliza, 'it's too cold to sit there.'

'Too cold!' said Mummy. 'It feels quite warm in here to me.'

'It's warm here,' said Darren, 'but not over there by the windows.'

So Mummy went to see, and sure enough she found a little gap between the floor and the long windows. 'There's a nasty cold draught coming in here,' she said. 'No wonder you felt cold. We must make a draught-excluder!'

'A draught-excluder!' said Darren. 'I don't think we can make one of those. It sounds very hard to make.'

'It's not difficult,' laughed Mummy. 'You'll see.' And she went upstairs to fetch some material and her sewing box.

Eliza and Darren watched as she cut two long, long pieces of material and sewed them together on her sewing machine.

'It looks like a snake,' cried Darren.

'That's right,' said Mummy, 'and now we must fill the snake up with stuffing. I've got some old nylon tights we can cut up.'

So the children carefully chopped up the old tights into little pieces and put them into the snake. Mummy gave Darren two black buttons to sew on for the snake's eyes and she gave Eliza a piece of red felt to make the snake a tongue.

When they had finished Mummy tied a piece of ribbon round the snake's neck. 'There,' she said, 'that's our draught-excluder finished.' And Mummy put the snake down on the floor underneath the windows.

'Now we can sit on the floor again,' said Eliza and Darren. 'Thank you, Mummy.'

87

Where's Teddy?

One day Daddy brought in three big boxes. 'It's time to put away your summer clothes and toys,' he said to Sharon and Clive. 'It's getting cold and you won't need them any more this year.'

Daddy piled everything into the three boxes and tied them up with string. Then he put them in the loft.

That night, when Clive was getting ready for bed, he suddenly said, 'Where's Teddy?'

He searched everywhere, and Sharon searched and Mummy and Daddy searched. But they couldn't find Teddy. So Clive had to go to bed without him and he was rather upset.

When he was finally asleep, Daddy said, 'I can't think where that bear is. We haven't been out today, so it must be in the house somewhere.'

'What did you do this afternoon while I was at work?' asked Mummy.

'Packed up the summer clothes,' said Daddy. Mummy smiled and Daddy groaned, 'Oh no, you don't think that Teddy got caught up in that lot?'

'I wouldn't be at all surprised,' said Mummy.

So Daddy had to go and get into the loft and undo the string and look through the boxes. He found Teddy at the bottom of the third box.

Daddy was rather cross but Clive was very pleased to wake up and find Teddy at the end of his bed.

Planting bulbs

One autumn morning Matthew's father said to him, 'I'm going to do some gardening today. Would you like to help me?'

'Yes, please,' said Matthew. 'I like gardening. What shall we do?'

'It's time to plant the bulbs, ready for when spring comes,' his father said.

So after breakfast Matthew put on his warm outdoor clothes and went into the garden. The bulbs were lying in a row on the grass. Some were big and brown, and others were small and yellow.

Matthew's father began to dig the holes for the bulbs to go into.

When there were enough holes, Matthew's father showed him how to plant the bulbs. And when Matthew had covered each one with soil, his father told him, 'Now the bulbs will lie in the ground until spring comes.'

'Then what will they do?' asked the little boy.

'Then they'll grow into flowers,' said his father. 'The garden is bare now, but in spring it will be full of colours – red and yellow and blue and white. All from the bulbs we've planted.'

'I'll like that,' said Matthew.

Jim's hero

The most famous person in the town where Jim lived, was Barry Langley. He was the captain of the local football team, and one of the best soccer players in the country. Other teams had offered thousands and thousands of pounds if he would play for them, but Barry stayed with his home-town club, and said that one day he hoped to lead them on to the field for the Cup Final.

When Jim and his friends played football in the park, Jim liked to pretend that he was Barry Langley, and tried to copy the way Barry ran, and swerved, and kicked – and the way he jumped for joy whenever his team scored a goal.

One day in the park, Jim was playing in goal, standing between the two pullovers which marked the goalposts. The rest of the players were all at the far end, crowding around the other goal. Jim knew they were going to score, and wished he was playing in the attack.

Suddenly, he saw a big man step into the middle of the group of children near the far goal. The man soon had the ball at his feet, and dodged past all the players, dribbling the ball down the field towards Jim.

Jim was annoyed – what right had a grown-up to come barging into their game like that, without even being asked? The tall figure approached him, and Jim stared hard at the ball, as the man steered it slowly forwards with skilful feet. It just wasn't fair – what could Jim do against a player who towered above him like a giant?

Angrily, Jim rushed at the ball and flung himself down on to it. The man tripped over, and fell on top of him. Then he got up, and picked Jim up off the ground in his strong arms.

'Are you all right, lad?' he asked.

Jim looked into his face, and gasped. It was Barry
Langley!

'I just thought I'd join in your game for a bit of fun,'
said Barry. 'I'm sorry if I hurt you.'

'No, no – I'm fine. Just fine!' said Jim.

'Well, you'll certainly make a fine footballer one day,'
said Barry. 'That was a brave tackle you did. What's your
name?'

'Jim.'

'Well, good luck, Jim! Be seeing you!'

Jim gazed after his hero, smiling, as the others gathered
round to congratulate him.

The Globs

Globs are great big, green, greedy space monsters. They fly
about the universe in green space ships looking for food.
Their favourite things to eat are fruit and trees and grass
and flowers. And they are very greedy. When they land on a
planet they eat absolutely all the fruit and trees and grass
and flowers there are. So it is not very nice to have a visit
from the Globs!

One day the Globs saw Planet Earth in the distance. 'That
looks a likely place,' said the Chief Glob, licking his
enormous lips.

So he sent two space ships down to Earth to see if there
was any food to be had. All the rest of the Globs waited up
in space licking their enormous lips.

At last one of the ships came back, and the Glob-in-
charge made her report. 'It's wonderful,' she said. 'We
landed in a warm sunny place where there are lots of trees
covered in fruit and lots of grass and lots of flowers.'

All the Globs licked their enormous lips and waited
impatiently for the second ship to come back. But when it
finally arrived the Globs inside were looking very gloomy.
'There's no food on that planet,' they said. 'Everything is

covered in some cold, hard, white stuff. There's no grass
and no flowers to be seen and all the trees look dead.'

The Globs couldn't understand it. Was this planet full
of food or wasn't it?

The Chief Glob decided to send two more ships down to
Earth to see what they could find. So they set off and the
first ship was soon back. 'Everything is growing,' reported
the Glob-in-charge. 'There is fresh green grass everywhere
and soon lots of flowers will be out.'

All the Globs cheered up and waited impatiently for the
second ship, licking their enormous lips.

The second ship was soon back – full of cross looking
Globs. 'Everything is dying,' they said. 'All the leaves are
falling off the trees and the flowers are dead.'

'It must be magic,' said the Chief Glob. 'There must be a
powerful magician on that planet. It is not safe for us to
land!'

So all the Globs flew away. It's lucky for us that Globs
don't understand that it's winter on one side of the Earth
while it's summer on the other, and that it's spring in some
countries while it's autumn in others!

A heap of leaves

One morning, Derek and his friend Jeremy went to play in the park. The park-keeper had been busy sweeping all the fallen leaves together into a big heap, ready for the lorry to take away.

For a while Derek and Jeremy played on the roundabout. Then Derek said, 'Let's go and play in the leaves.'

So they did. First they climbed up on top of the heap and jumped down again. Then they pretended to be aeroplanes, flying round and round and diving into the leaves. And when they were tired of that, they kicked the leaves into the air and threw them at each other.

'What's going on here?' a voice asked suddenly. It was the park-keeper! 'What a mess you've made of my tidy heap,' he told the boys. 'You'd better help me to sweep all these leaves up again before the lorry comes.'

So Derek and Jeremy helped the park-keeper to sweep up. And when the lorry arrived, the keeper let them help to load the leaves on to the back of the lorry.

And then there was just time to put the broom and the rake away in the keeper's shed before they had to go home.

Bernie badger

Mother Badger called her family together. 'Winter is nearly here,' she said. 'It is time for our big sleep.'

'What sleep?' asked Bernie, the eldest. His mother told him how they slept until spring, and it was called 'hibernation'.

Bernie was horrified. 'Sleep all that time?' he gasped. 'But I might miss something!' And he firmly refused to hibernate at all. He went to find the hedgehogs to ask them to play. But they were curled in tight, prickly balls – and snoring. The squirrels were fast asleep, too.

'*I'm* not tired,' said Bernie. But as the days passed he yawned and felt lonely.

Then, the first snowflakes began to fall. 'What's this?' he wondered. He gazed up at the swirling flakes, and they stuck on his nose. Before he knew it, he was as white as the world around him.

He didn't like it, and rushed home. 'Just until this white stuff goes,' he told himself, as he crept inside.

Mother Badger shook him. 'Wake up!' she said.

Bernie blinked, then remembered. 'I'm white!' he cried. 'Everything is white!'

They all laughed at him. 'You're dreaming!'

He peeped outside . . . and saw it was springtime.

He had hibernated after all!

The apple farm

Early one morning, Colin was woken by a loud noise
underneath his bedroom window. He pulled back the curtain
and looked out. There in the street was a red lorry.

Colin rushed downstairs to tell his father. 'The apple
lorry is here! It's waiting to take us to the apple farm!'

'Come and eat your breakfast first,' said his mother.

So Colin ate his breakfast, very quickly, and washed and
dressed himself and ran outside. Waiting beside the lorry
was a little stout man with a round red face. 'Are you Mr
Green the apple farmer?' Colin asked him.

'That's right,' said the man. 'Up you get into my lorry
now, and off we'll go.'

So Colin and his mother and father got in and the red lorry drove out of the town and far into the countryside. At last it stopped at the apple farm. Everywhere there were trees covered with ripe, juicy apples, and children helping their parents to pick the apples and put them into big round baskets.

Mr Green showed them from which tree they were to take the fruit. It had so many apples on it that the branches bowed down to the grass.

Colin's mother and father started to pick the apples and gave them to him to put into a basket. Then, when the bottom branches were empty, Colin's father put a ladder against the tree and helped Colin to climb up to reach the apples on the top branches. Soon the basket was full.

While his father had a rest, Colin played with the other children. They chased each other in and out of the apple trees and played hide and seek in the barn where the farmer kept his red lorry.

At the end of the day Colin was very tired. Mr Green the farmer took them home again in his lorry, and he gave Colin a whole box of ripe juicy apples for himself. But Colin wasn't sure that he wanted them. He had had quite enough of apples for one day!

The castle ghost

There was a ruined castle near the village where Donald and Jean lived, and a ghost was said to roam among the stone walls, moaning and groaning.

One cold, dark evening, Donald and Jean dared each other to go to the castle! They pretended to be very brave as they climbed the gate into the field where the ruins stood. The walls loomed up black and unfriendly against the sky, and the wind seemed to whisper in the dark corners.

'Perhaps there isn't any ghost,' said Jean.

'Even if there is,' said Donald, 'I'm not scared of it!'

'Nor am I!' said Jean.

'Then why are you shivering?' asked Donald.

'I'm cold, that's all,' Jean said. 'Besides, you're shivering too.'

'No, I'm not,' said Donald.

'Yes, you are,' Jean persisted.

'No, I'm not,' said Donald.

'Shush!' whispered Jean suddenly. 'Listen! I thought I heard footsteps.'

They clutched each other and listened. Sure enough, someone, or something, was treading heavily on the grass, just behind the wall where they stood.

'It's the ghost!' whispered Donald. 'What shall we do?'

'Stay quite still,' said Jean. 'It may go away again without seeing us.'

Just then, from behind the wall, came a terrifying sound, like a loud, deep moan.

Donald and Jean gasped, and started to run, through the ruins and across the field. They scrambled over the gate and ran and ran, until they fell in at the door of their parents' cottage.

'Whatever have you two been doing?' asked their mother.

'We were just having a race,' gasped Donald.

'Well, get yourselves washed, and I'll give you some tea,' said their mother.

When they were ready for tea, their father came in and said he'd just met Farmer Moffatt, bringing back one of his cows that had strayed into the castle.

'Mr Moffatt said it was mooing away as if it was really upset,' said their father. 'He wondered if it had seen the ghost!'

He laughed. Donald and Jean looked at each other. So *that* was what they had heard – Farmer Moffatt's cow, tramping about, and then starting to moo. They began to join in the laughter. . . .

The grey squirrel

One day last autumn, when Laura and her mother were taking their dog Paddy for a walk in the wood, they saw a grey squirrel. It was sitting under a tree, nibbling at a nut.

'Wuff!' barked Paddy loudly. 'Wuff-wuff!' And he tried to chase the squirrel, but it ran up the tree trunk and hid safely on a branch.

'Naughty Paddy,' said Laura. 'You mustn't frighten the poor squirrel away.'

'It's time for him to collect all the nuts he can find for his winter larder,' said Laura's mother, 'or he won't have anything to eat when the snow comes.'

'Why don't we help the squirrel?' asked Laura. 'We can look for nuts and leave them for him at the bottom of this tree.'

So she and her mother began to search. Paddy thought it was a game and ran backwards and forwards, barking. Soon their pockets were full of nuts and they carried them back to the squirrel's tree.

The little grey squirrel looked down at them from his branch. 'I think he's saying "thank you",' said Laura.

The mist monster

It was a very misty morning. The mist was so thick that when Sally looked through her window she couldn't see the garden at all. 'It's like being in the middle of a cloud,' she thought.

After breakfast, she put on her warm anorak and went out to play on the lawn. First of all, she pretended that she was a bird, flying through the clouds. Then she pretended that she was invisible. And then she pretended that she was lost in a strange, misty world.

Suddenly, Sally stopped. There in front of her stood an enormous grey shadow with long bare arms reaching out to grab her! It must be a mist monster!

'What do you want?' the little girl shouted. But the mist monster didn't answer.

Sally felt scared but she went closer. The monster had a long grey body and knobbly, wrinkled skin. And it stood very still.

But then, slowly, something began to move along the monster's shoulder. Sally stared. It was her cat, Clea.

'Clea!' she shouted, and ran to rescue her from the mist monster. And then she saw what the mist monster really was. It was the tree at the bottom of the garden.

Sally began to laugh. Fancy being frightened of a tree!

Cold spells

One day the wizard found none of his spells would work. He had a spell to make the kettle boil which he used in the morning to make his cup of tea, but that wouldn't work. He had a spell which made toast for his breakfast, but that wouldn't work either.

'Whatever is the matter!' he said crossly. 'It's very cold today and I need a nice hot cup of tea and a lovely piece of hot, buttered toast. I can't understand it.'

In the end he had to go and ask the advice of the witch who lived next door.

'That is strange,' she said, when the wizard had explained what was the matter. 'I'll look in my spell book and see if I can find a spell to cure spells that won't work.'

She walked over to the shelf to fetch her spell book. Her big black cat was sitting right on top of it. 'That's right, Puss,' she said. 'You sit up there and keep my spells warm.'

The big black cat stretched and yawned and purred.

'How do you keep your spells warm in this cold weather?' the witch asked the wizard.

'How do I keep my spells warm!' said the wizard in amazement. 'Why should I do that?'

'Don't you know that spells have to be kept warm?' said the witch in surprise. 'The cat keeps my spells warm. He sleeps on top of my spell book. If spells get cold they won't work at all.'

'Oh dear,' said the wizard. 'That's what is wrong with my spells then. I didn't know they had to be kept warm. I haven't been a wizard very long. I only passed my wizard exams in the summer.'

'Goodness me,' said the witch. 'I don't know what they teach you at wizard school these days. Fancy not knowing that you must keep your spells warm.'

'What can I do?' asked the wizard. 'Wizards don't have cats.'

'I tell you what,' said the witch. 'I'll lend you my everlasting hot water bottle to put on top of your spell book until you can get down to the magic shop and buy one for yourself.'

So the wizard's spells worked again, and the first spell he did was to magic up a big bunch of roses to give to the witch next door.

Looking for things

William was bored. It was a windy autumn day and he had nothing to do. He had played with his toys. He had looked through a picture book. He had been out into the garden with his dog Cindy. 'What *am* I going to do for the rest of the day?' he asked his mother.

'Would you like to come for a walk with me?' she suggested.

William frowned. 'But walks are boring, too,' he said crossly.

His mother smiled. 'Why don't we take Cindy to the park? You can look for things to take to school tomorrow.'

'What sort of things?' William wanted to know.

'Come with me and I'll show you,' his mother told him.

So William put on his duffel coat and his red woolly hat, his scarf and gloves and shiny new wellingtons. And when he was ready, he and his mother walked with Cindy to the park.

'Now,' said his mother, 'Let's see how many things we can find to put on the nature table in your classroom tomorrow.'

'That's a good idea!' said William. 'I'd forgotten about the nature table.'

So they began to look around the park. William found five big brown acorns in their little cups. And after that he found an empty snail shell.

William's mother gathered up all the pretty leaves she could find – brown leaves and red leaves, orange and yellow and copper-coloured leaves. And Cindy found a branch that the wind had blown down that was covered with bright red berries.

At last William's mother said, 'We must go home for lunch now.'

'Oh, *must* we?' asked William. He didn't want to go home just yet. He was having such fun.

'If you like, ' said his mother, 'you can come back to the park this afternoon with Daddy.'

So, after they had had their meal, William went with his father and Cindy to look for more things for the nature table.

William's father found an empty bird's nest and a long brown feather. And William found a heap of little beech-nuts still inside their green prickly cases. And Cindy found a very old bone.

When it began to grow dark, they went home for tea. And later, when he was tucked up in bed, William decided that he'd been *far* too busy to be bored.

The moon and stars

One night it was cold and frosty and the sky was very clear.
Rosemary could see all the stars and she could see a great
big yellow moon floating in the sky as well.

'The moon looks like a great big yellow balloon,' she said
to her mother. 'Can I buy a big yellow balloon tomorrow?'
she asked. 'Then I can have a moon of my own.'

'Of course,' said Mummy.

So next day when they went out shopping, Rosemary
bought a big yellow balloon. When they got home Mummy
blew it up.

'I wish I had some stars as well,' said Rosemary.

'I know,' said Mummy, 'you can cut some stars out of my
kitchen foil.'

So Rosemary hung the balloon in one corner of her
bedroom and stuck some silver stars on the walls.

'Now I've got my own moon and stars,' she said.

The fly-away kite

Martin had a new kite. It was a bright yellow one, with a long blue tail, and when Martin flew the kite it soared high up into the air and zig-zagged and swooped and went round and round in circles.

Onė wild, windy autumn day, Martin went out with his father to fly his new kite. Up it went into the sky, tugging at the string. Martin held on tightly, then, suddenly, he tripped over a tree root and let go of the string. And away went his kite, swooping and circling and zig-zagging over the field. Martin and his father ran after it, but they couldn't catch it.

'Never mind,' said his father, 'I'll buy you another one.'
'But that was my best one,' sobbed Martin.

Sadly, they went home. But when Martin opened the garden gate, he couldn't believe his eyes. Because there, caught in the branches of the tree next door, was his kite!

'Look! It's come home all by itself,' he told his father. 'The wind must have shown it the way.'

The lonely beach

One weekend in autumn Ashley and Caroline went to stay
with their grandparents at the seaside.

'Would you like to go for a walk on the beach?' their
grandfather asked them.

'Can we paddle in the sea?' asked Ashley.

'Can we build a sandcastle?' asked Caroline.

'Oh no,' replied their grandmother. 'The sea is much too
cold now that autumn has come. And the sand is too wet
for building sandcastles.'

'Then what can we do?' asked the children.

'Wait and see,' said their grandparents.

It was a chilly, windy afternoon. Caroline and Ashley put
on their coats and scarves and gloves, their woolly hats and
their wellingtons, and set off down to the beach.

'It looks so lonely without people,' Caroline said.

'I like it,' said Ashley and he picked up a pebble and
threw it as far as he could along the sand. 'You can't throw

pebbles when people are here.'

'Come along,' called their grandparents. 'Let's go and see what the sea has washed up on the sand.' So they walked down to the edge of the waves and began to search among the green seaweed there.

Ashley found a big white shell and a gull's feather. And then he found a long piece of rope. Caroline found a pretty bottle and an empty crab shell. And their grandmother found a red rubber ball.

They played at skipping with the rope. And when they were nice and warm they threw the ball to each other. Then their grandfather found a smooth piece of wood.

'Let's have a game of cricket,' he said. 'This wood can be the bat.'

So Ashley and Caroline took it in turns to play. Ashley hit the ball high into the air, but his grandfather caught it and so it was Caroline's turn. She missed the ball twice, but then she knocked it so far that Ashley had to run and run before he could stop it.

'The wind is getting too cold for us to play now,' said their grandmother. 'Let's shelter behind the sand dunes.'

So they did. The dunes had steep sides and the twins played on them, running up to the top and sliding all the way down to the bottom.

Then it was time to go home. 'We'll come again tomorrow,' promised their grandparents. 'Would you like that?'

'Yes *please*,' said Ashley and Caroline. 'There's so much to do on this lonely beach!'

Back-to-front land

Philip was very excited. Today was the day he and his
parents were flying in an aeroplane. They were going to
stay with Philip's uncle, who lived on the other side of the
world in a country called New Zealand.

They drove in the car to the airport, and on the way
Philip looked out of the window. It was autumn now, and all
the trees were bare. There were no flowers in the gardens.
Everyone wore their warmest coats and gloves because the
wind was so cold. The sky was grey and big black clouds hid
the sun. 'Brr,' said Philip. 'I'll be glad when springtime
comes.'

At the airport, the little boy and his parents got into a big
plane. The plane began to move, going faster and faster
until it went up into the air and away over the tops of the
houses.

The plane journey lasted a long, long time. But at last they reached New Zealand, where Philip's uncle lived. When they got off the plane, his uncle was waiting for them in his car and he drove them to his house.

Philip looked out through the car window. 'That's strange,' he thought to himself. 'Whatever has happened to autumn?' Here in New Zealand, the trees were covered with green leaves. The gardens were full of flowers. No one was wearing coats and gloves. And up above, the sky was blue and the sun shone warmly down.

Philip was very puzzled. 'Why has the weather changed?' he asked his uncle. 'When we got into the aeroplane it was autumn. But now, suddenly, spring is here. The plane journey must have taken a *very* long time!'

His uncle laughed. 'Don't worry, Philip,' he said. 'It's still autumn at home where you live. But here it's springtime.'

'I see,' said Philip thoughtfully. 'So everything is upside down and back-to-front on the other side of the world?'

'I suppose it is,' laughed his uncle.

'I've never had a back-to-front holiday before,' said Philip. 'This *is* going to be fun!'

The old clock

In Celia's granny's old house, in the draughty panelled hall, stood a very, very old grandfather clock. It had belonged to granny's family for more than two hundred years.

One winter Celia was staying with her granny and every day, as the weather became colder, the clock began to creak and groan as if to say, 'Brr, I'm cold. I don't want to work, I just want to sleep.' And it began to stop working. It got slower and slower.

'Winter's nearly here now,' said Granny.

'How do you know?' Celia asked.

'Just wait and see,' Granny replied.

One night it snowed heavily and the wind whistled down the chimney in Celia's room. Next morning Granny said, 'Winter's here – come and look.' They went out into the hall and Granny pointed to the old clock. 'Look,' she said. 'The old clock has stopped completely.'

'Is it broken for ever?' asked Celia.

'Oh no,' said Granny. 'Every year it stops when winter comes, and then when spring is on the way it comes to life again, very slowly day by day. It tells me when I can start thinking of summery things.'

'It's a bit like a hedgehog hibernating, isn't it?' said Celia.

The holly

It was rather sad in the garden. All the flowers were dead. All the trees had lost their leaves. Everything was brown and ugly.

Lynne looked at her father. 'There's nothing nice here,' she said. 'There are no flowers to pick. There aren't even any pretty coloured leaves left to put in Mummy's vase. They've all fallen off the trees.'

'Look carefully in that corner,' said her father.

Lynne looked and saw something green. She ran over and found a tree which hadn't lost its leaves. It had some bright red berries as well.

'That's pretty,' said Lynne and reached out her hand to touch the tree.

'Careful!' said her father. 'That's holly and the leaves have got lots of prickles.'

'Why haven't the leaves fallen off this tree?' asked Lynne.

'Because holly is an evergreen,' said her father. 'Some trees are called evergreens because their leaves don't all fall off in the autumn. I will pick some holly with berries on for you, so you will have something pretty to put in Mummy's vase after all.'

again

...ng Mr Robinson took his children to school and every morning Mr Robinson, Brian Robinson, Angela Robinson and Judith Robinson rushed out of the house at the last minute. They were always late!

One morning the Robinsons were even later than usual. It was a very cold morning and none of the children wanted to get out of bed. It was so cold outside the bedclothes.

When they did get up they discovered that their mother had made some lovely hot porridge. But the porridge was *so* hot it took a long time to eat.

When they all finally tumbled out of the house they were already ten minutes later than they should have been. Mr Robinson rushed up to his car. But when he saw it he gave a great big groan. 'Oh no,' he said, 'just look at the car. It will take ages to get the windows clear.' For the windows were all white with frost.

At last Mr Robinson finished scraping off the frost and they all jumped into the car. But it was so cold that the car didn't want to start. It just made a horrible clanking noise. It made such a loud noise that Mr James over the road came out to see what was happening. 'I think we better give you a push,' he said.

So the children jumped out and they and Mr James pushed the car down the road as fast as they could. At last the engine started.

Of course by then the children were so late for school that Mr Robinson had to take them in and apologize to their teacher. The teacher was rather cross!

When the children got home that evening they saw a strange grey shape outside their house. From a distance it looked just like an elephant sitting down. But when the children got nearer they could see it was a great big grey plastic sheet with something underneath.

'It's a winter coat for the car,' explained Mr Robinson, 'and I've bought something else too – a great big alarm clock to wake us all up. We are not going to be late again. I'm too scared of your teacher!'

The red dress

Daisy had a red dress which she loved to wear. She liked it so much that she wanted to wear it all the time, although of course she couldn't because sometimes it had to be washed. But she did wear it as often as she could.

The trouble was that Daisy's red dress was a summer dress. The material was quite thin and it had short sleeves. When the summer was over and it began to get cold, Daisy's mummy said, 'Daisy, you can't wear that dress today. It's not warm enough.'

'Oh please Mummy,' said Daisy, 'I will be warm enough. I will wear a cardigan over it.'

'All right,' said Daisy's mother. 'As long as you are warm enough.'

But soon it got much colder, and Daisy's mother said, 'Daisy, you really can't wear that dress today. It's not warm enough.'

'Oh please Mummy,' said Daisy, 'I'll wear a vest under it and a cardigan over it.'

'All right,' said her mother. 'As long as you are quite sure that you are warm enough.'

But then it got even colder, and Daisy's mother said,
'Daisy, I can't let you wear that dress today.'

'Oh please Mummy,' said Daisy, 'I'll wear my woolly
tights and my vest and a cardigan.'

So Daisy was allowed to wear the dress that day! But the
very next day it snowed. Daisy's mother came into her
bedroom. Daisy looked sad. 'I suppose I can't wear my
favourite dress today as it's snowing.'

'No you can't,' said Mummy, 'so it's lucky I've made you
this new red dress out of some nice warm material.'

Mummy held up a beautiful red dress exactly the same
colour as Daisy's favourite summer dress.

'Now I've got a favourite winter dress, too,' Daisy smiled.

The polar mouse

Lawrence's toy mouse, Joey, had a clockwork motor inside him. When Lawrence wound him up, Joey went round in circles, making a whirring noise.

One morning, Lawrence discovered that a puddle of water on the garden path was frozen over. A stone was sticking up from the ice, like a tiny mountain. Lawrence thought it looked like the scenery at the North Pole.

'Joey,' he said, 'how would you like to be a polar mouse?' He put Joey down on the frozen puddle, and Joey went round and round, sliding a bit on the ice. Then he hit the stone and turned over on his side, still whirring. Lawrence thought he sounded quite angry.

'Don't worry, Joey,' he called, 'the Polar Rescue Team is here!' He reached out and grabbed Joey, but his hand went through the ice, and when he brought it out his fingers were cold and wet – and so was Joey!

Lawrence's mother dried Joey with a towel, and when Lawrence wound him up, he went round and round just as happily as before.

'No more trips to the North Pole,' Lawrence promised. 'You won't have to be a polar mouse ever again!'

Patch's coat

Stephanie lived next door to an old lady called Mrs Scott. Mrs Scott had a dog called Patch and Stephanie often took him for a walk.

One morning Stephanie called at Mrs Scott's door. 'Would Patch like to come out for a walk?' she asked.

'That's very kind of you dear,' said Mrs Scott. 'But I'm afraid it's rather cold out for poor Patch. You see, he is a very old dog and I'm afraid he feels the cold a lot. Perhaps you can take him out when it's warmer.'

Stephanie went home and told her parents about poor Patch.

'I've got an idea,' said her mother. 'I'll knit Patch a coat.' And she knitted a coat out of all her leftover scraps of wool.

The next day Stephanie went to see Mrs Scott again. 'Hello Stephanie,' Mrs Scott said. 'Have you come to take Patch for a walk? I'm afraid it's still too cold for him. He'll have to make do with a run in the garden.'

'I've brought Patch a present,' said Stephanie, and showed Mrs Scott the coat.

'Well,' said Mrs Scott, 'that is kind of you. Now Patch can go out for a walk after all.'

The typhoon

On the South Sea Islands, they use banana leaves for skirts.

Tia, a little native girl, set out to fetch some fresh ones.
'I remember where there are some good, wild bananas,' she
thought, as she ran down to the creek to fetch her canoe.
The creek ran through a mangrove swamp to the sea, and
she pushed out her small canoe and glided through the water.

Here grew a jungle of trees and palms, dark and
mysterious. It was cool, which Tia liked, for though it was
winter, it is always warm in the South Seas.

From the greenery surrounding her, came the chattering
of monkeys, and the calling of brightly coloured birds.

She pulled the canoe out of the water, and, walking into
the sunshine again, found the banana trees.

Some other children were already there. They were all
wearing necklaces like Tia's, made of shells or seeds.

'I need some new leaves,' she told them. Chatting and
friendly, they helped her find some.

Then, carrying the bundle, she went back to the canoe
and paddled away. It was a while before she realized
something was strange. 'Where are the monkeys?' she
wondered. It was deadly quiet. No monkeys, no birds,
nothing.

Then, the wind began to blow. She trembled. These were
the signs that a typhoon was coming!

She knew she must get out of the water. For a terrible
rainstorm would be blowing in from the sea.

Finding a place to land, she dragged the canoe high behind the undergrowth. Then, she quickly pulled it over herself, peeping from underneath.

She had never been alone in a storm before.

Across the darkened sky flashed light, sometimes red, sometimes green.

Tia stared at the sight of her lovely creek. It became a mass of huge waves. Then came the rain, lashing the palm trees almost to the ground.

Tia shivered, and curled herself up inside her shelter.

When the storm had finally blown out, Tia set off through the dripping leaves for home.

There, it was a terrible sight. Along the beach, trees were uprooted, and many of the palm-thatched huts were wrecked.

The people were grouped around staring at the damage. Tia's mother saw her.

'Tia!' she cried. 'Where have you been?' She clasped her tightly. 'But, you are dry! Where *did* you shelter in such a storm?'

'Under my canoe!' laughed Tia.

And her mother was so happy that she was safe.

Eskimo Jobee

In the winter, the Eskimos move into huts built partly underground. But the Eskimo fur-trappers have to spend winter away from their families.

Jobee watched his father, Senach, prepare for winter trapping.

'I could come and help,' said Jobee.

His father shook his head. 'Boys hunt at twelve years, not before.'

Tears pricked Jobee's eyes. He hated it when his father went away. He watched him pile the sledge with food and blankets.

Jobee was determined, that this time, he would join him.

The next day Senach began his journey. He trekked over the frozen sea, towards white, pointed mountains and his winter cabin. There, he unpacked.

At the bottom of the sledge, a round-eyed little face looked up at him from its fur hood. 'Jobee!' cried his father.

Jobee climbed out.

'You must go back!' snapped his father.

Jobee stared with fright, and looked back through the white forest.

His father sighed. He knew that was impossible. 'All right,' he shrugged. 'You will have to stay.'

Jobee's pinky-brown face lit with smiles.

When Senach hunted, Jobee stayed in the cabin. The bitter wind would rage outside, and even the drinking water would freeze in its pan. It stayed dark all the time; there was no daylight.

One day some wild animal came snuffling around the door. Jobee took hold of a gun, trembling, ready. He was still holding it when his father returned.

Next day, Senach said, 'You come with me. I will teach
you to trap.'

They worked hard for many days. Then, when a low,
silver sun began to break the darkness, Senach said, 'I have
more furs than ever before! We must build a canoe to take
them back. It will make the journey easier.'

As they made the canoe, the sunlight began casting long
shadows on the ice. Soon, the thaw set free the frozen lakes
and streams.

They packed the canoe, and Senach placed Jobee in
front of him. Jobee was now very tired.

He watched the moving mountains with sleepy eyes, as
they sped through the water.

'I think,' he said, 'I will wait until I'm older, before I
come again.'

'I think,' smiled Senach, 'that is wise. I will look forward
to the time when you can come with me.'

Nicola's hat

Not long ago Nicola's granny knitted her a new hat. It was a woolly red hat with a big pom-pom, and Nicola was very proud of it.

The first time she wore it was on a cold and windy day. Nicola didn't mind the weather. 'My new woolly hat will keep me nice and warm,' she said, and she went outside to play.

The wind rushed along the street towards her, blowing leaves and paper into the air. It whistled round the corner, making doors slam. It pulled at Nicola's coat and blew her scarf about.

Then the wind tried to snatch the new woolly hat. First it blew one way, then it blew another. It huffed and puffed and tried to push the hat over her eyes. Then it puffed and huffed and tried to pull it backwards off her head. But it couldn't blow Nicola's hat away.

'Silly wind,' Nicola said. 'What's the use of blowing so hard? You'll make yourself tired. You can't blow *my* hat off!'

The winter flood

Roger and Joanne lived by a river, and, if it rained a lot, the river would get deeper and run faster.

One winter night, it absolutely poured with rain.

'Listen,' whispered Joanne. 'It sounds as if we are under a waterfall.'

They awoke next morning, to hear Daddy shouting. 'The river – it's burst its banks!'

They leapt out of bed, and stood on the landing, staring. The water was lapping up the stairs.

'Stay there!' shouted Daddy, sloshing about in pyjamas and wellingtons. He and Mummy were stacking the furniture into piles and carrying it upstairs.

The children felt quite excited. They looked out of the bedroom windows, and saw water everywhere. Later on, a neighbour came to the door – by boat! He called, 'Is there anything you need?'

'We're all right, thank you!' said Daddy.

'Would the children like to come with me for a ride, then?' asked the neighbour.

So Roger and Joanne had a ride across the water. It was funny to row up to windows and to find trees growing out of the water. They were really quite sorry when the water all disappeared!

'Well no one else is!' said Mummy. 'We are only too glad to get the house dry again!'

Donkey rescue

Gino was very happy. He was going to visit his cousin Peta
all by himself. Gino and Peta lived in Italy, high up in the
mountains. Gino lived in a little village on one side of a
mountain and Peta lived in a village on the other.

The sun was shining and the snow sparkled on the
pathway over the little mountain. Gino was not alone.
Walking beside him was his grey donkey, Julietta. She was
happy too – she had just had an enormous feed. Gino sung
as he walked and Julietta hee-hawed to show that she liked
Gino's singing. Neither of them were looking at the pathway.
Suddenly Gino screamed. His foot had slipped off the
pathway and into a little gulley filled with snow. He wasn't
in pain but his foot was stuck fast.

'O Julietta, what am I going to do?' Gino said. 'No one may come this way all day and I'm already getting cold.' Julietta hee-hawed to show she understood and then suddenly trotted off over the mountain path and disappeared.

'Oh don't leave me Julietta,' cried Gino. 'Where are you going?' But she had gone. Gino was very sad and worried and cried a little. He tugged at his foot but it wouldn't move at all.

It seemed to Gino that he had been there a long time when he heard footsteps on the pathway. 'Help, I'm here, help me,' he cried. Suddenly, over the crest of the little mountain, Julietta appeared. Gino couldn't believe his eyes for sitting on her back was his cousin Peta with Uncle Dino following close behind.

'Well young man, you have got yourself in a fix haven't you?' said Uncle Dino. 'But don't worry we'll soon have you out.'

Slowly, he lifted the rock which was trapping Gino's foot. Uncle Dino felt Gino's foot carefully. 'No bones broken,' he said. 'Have a drink of this to warm you up.' In a flask he had some steaming hot, sweet chocolate.

'But how did you know where I was?' said Gino.

'A certain grey donkey came trotting up our path,' said Uncle Dino. 'She made such a racket that we had to follow her.'

'O Julietta, thank you,' said Gino, planting a big kiss on her shaggy mane.

Skating

Cathy jumped out of bed, and pulled back the curtains. The window was so frozen, she couldn't see out at all.

She pressed her warm fingers on the pane and made peepholes.

Everything was white with thick frost. The shallow river running by their home was still and hard.

She ran downstairs. 'Look at the weather!' she cried. 'The river is frozen!'

'I know,' said Mummy. 'Daddy is outside with Stephen, testing it.'

Stephen was Cathy's elder brother. He came dashing in, cheeks glowing, eyes bright.

'It's solid, Mummy!' he said excitedly. 'Where are my skates?'

'*I* want to skate,' said Cathy.

Daddy came in, stamping his feet. 'It's safe enough,' he said. 'In fact, some neighbours are skating already.'

'*I* want to skate!' cried Cathy, again.

'You're too little,' said Stephen.

'No I'm not!' Cathy was cross. 'Not this year!'

'Well you haven't any skates!' said Stephen, finding his. But when he tried them on – they wouldn't fit him anymore!

'Never mind,' said Daddy. 'I'll try to get you some, later.'

'I'll have to slide with my wellingtons,' said Stephen.

But the skates fitted Cathy – with two pairs of socks, that is. She could hardly wait to start skating.

They both went outside. Cathy gasped. The air was so keen, and the world around so beautiful. It was like a white wonderland.

People were skating quickly along, dressed in warm, bright clothes, with scarves flying.

Stephen joined them, sliding about. 'Wait for me!' cried Cathy. She copied the others, pushing her feet across the ice. And fell.

She tried again. And sat down with a thump. Stephen thought it a huge joke. No matter how Cathy tried, she could *not* skate.

After a while, Stephen, still laughing, ran off.

Cathy tried again, then stayed down, disheartened.

Suddenly, a bicycle came along – someone was riding a bicycle on the river! It was Stephen.

'Stand up,' he said, 'and hold on to the bike. I'll *pull* you along!'

So Cathy skated after all. She hung on tight, and they whizzed past the other skaters.

They had a lovely time. 'We're the fastest pair on ice!' they laughed.

The snowman

The garden was covered with a white blanket of snow.
Michelle came to play with Sonia. They ran all over the
white blanket, making footprints everywhere. The snow
nearly went over their wellingtons!

They snowballed each other, and chased around, then
stopped for breath.

'Let's make a snowman,' said Michelle.

They rolled snow into a huge ball, then made a smaller
ball on top of it. They found two stones for eyes, and a twig
for a mouth.

Sonia's mummy gave them an old scarf and hat, and even
a carrot for his nose. He was a splendid snowman.

Next morning, Sonia rushed to her window to see him
again. The snowman had gone!

She hurriedly dressed and went outside to look. To her
astonishment, the snowman was there – but in a different
place! She fetched Michelle. Michelle stared, too. She said
eventually, 'The snowman, must have *walked*!'

They gazed at each other with round eyes, and decided to
keep the secret to themselves.

That night, Daddy said to Mummy, 'It's funny that
Sonia hasn't asked about the snowman. I couldn't get the
car out, so I had to move him out of the way.'

'Perhaps,' said Mummy, 'she hasn't noticed.'

The sledge ride

Christopher lived in a very flat part of the countryside, where there wasn't a hill in sight. That made sledging difficult! But one year when the snow came, he had the longest, fastest sledge ride, ever.

'Come on!' his daddy said. 'Into the car with the sledge!' And he took Christopher – and his dog – to the top of a river bank. There was a track here, which led to their farm. Only Christopher's parents used it so it was very quiet.

Daddy tied the sledge to the back of the car with strong rope. 'Sit tight, then!' he called, and off they went, slowly down the track.

One day, Mummy came along in the car to watch. 'This is fun!' she said, and turned round to wave to Christopher. 'Stop!' she cried. 'We're pulling an empty sledge!' Christopher and his dog were nowhere to be seen.

'We can't turn until the track ends!' exclaimed Daddy.

When they got back, they found Christopher, sitting with the dog, waiting.

'What happened?' asked Daddy.

'I was pulling my woolly hat down,' Christopher giggled, 'so as you started – I fell off!'

Persis and Rahul

Persis and Rahul were leaving India to join their mother and father in England. Auntie Indira packed for them and saw them off and gave them into the care of a children's officer on board a ship sailing to England. Persis and Rahul were sorry to leave but they had a wonderful time on the ship. It was very hot as they sailed around the Cape of Good Hope and they spent every day in the beautiful swimming pool.

When they crossed the Equator, there was a big party on board, and everyone dressed in funny clothes and threw each other into the swimming pool. Persis and Rahul loved every minute.

As they travelled up the coast of Africa a strange thing happened. The warm winter weather disappeared and it

became colder and colder. Persis and Rahul had never known such cold. They took clothes out of their suitcase they had never worn before – their father had sent them. Trousers and jumpers and funny padded coats called anoraks. The swimming pool was closed and the sea turned from blue to grey.

At last the day came when they were due to dock in Liverpool and they could hardly wait to see their mother and father again.

'Do you think they will know us?' said Rahul to Persis, for he was a very little boy and a year seemed a long time to him.

'Of course,' said Persis, 'don't be stupid.'

As the big ship docked Persis and Rahul stared over the side. They had never seen anything like it. Every flat surface was white, and flakes of white were falling everywhere. Rahul was not sure he liked it.

Suddenly Persis screamed, 'There's Daddy!' And five minutes later their father was hugging them both.

'I thought you might not recognize us,' said Rahul.

'I recognized you all right,' said his father, 'but I wondered if you would know me, dressed like this.' He was covered from head to toe in fur – a furry hat and coat and big boots with fur sides.

'You look like a bear,' said Rahul and smiled, happy to be with his father again, even in such a funny cold country.

Snowed-up Saturday

Katie rushed into her parents' room. 'The house is buried under snow!' she cried.

Daddy jumped out of bed. The window was blocked with snow, but it opened easily. 'You are a goose,' he said. 'The wind has blown snow on to the windows!' He laughed at her. 'Mind you, it must have snowed a lot.'

It certainly had. The outside world had vanished into a white wilderness.

'We didn't expect this!' exclaimed Mummy. 'It's Saturday, too. We shall be without milk all weekend.'

'I'll go to the dairy,' said Daddy. 'The tractor should get through.'

'Can I come?' asked Katie, excited.

When they were ready, Katie opened the door. She couldn't get out! The snow was piled as high as she was.

Daddy pushed his way through, then put Katie on his shoulders, and made his way to the tractor shed.

He fastened a big snowplough to the tractor front.

'We had better take a spade,' he said. 'Jump on, Katie!'

They set off towards the village, ploughing through the snow. Here and there were empty cars, buried in the drifts.

The village was a sight to see. The snow had blown high up against the houses, and long icicles hung from the roofs. People heard the tractor, and leaned out of their upstairs windows, calling. Daddy jumped out to talk to them.

'They all need milk!' he told Katie. 'And bread, too, for the weekend. So we'll go to the bakery as well.'

'It's a long way,' said Katie.

'We'll make it!' Daddy laughed.

They had quite a struggle up a hilly part. Then, 'Look!' shouted Katie, 'poor Mrs Burns' cottage!' Down a lane, the little cottage had almost disappeared under the snow.

Daddy turned the tractor, and it pushed its way towards the cottage. Then, with the spade, Katie's father cleared a way to the door.

'I'm *so* glad to see you!' said the old lady, thankfully. 'I thought I would be snowed up for days!'

She needed milk and bread, too. So, on the way back, Mrs Burns was the first they delivered to. She gave them a hot drink to warm them up.

In the village, everyone was now shovelling snow. They waved and cheered as the tractor returned.

Katie handed out the milk and bread, and thoroughly enjoyed herself. Then they set off back home.

'I've been so worried!' Mummy said. 'It's taken you hours to fetch me some milk!'

Delivering the post

In Canada, the rivers and great lakes are covered with snow and ice almost half the year.

But Carrie-Ann had not played in the snow this winter. She had been ill for a long time.

'Can I get you anything?' her Mummy asked, anxious about the pale, ill face.

Carrie-Ann shook her head, and gazed sadly out towards the forest. In the distance, something was moving. It was the mailman with his dog-team and sledge, coming nearer. He brought them a letter.

'How's our invalid today?' he asked.

'Too pale,' sighed Mummy.

The mailman stared at Carrie-Ann. 'Let her come with me,' he said. 'She could help me by sorting the letters out.'

So Carrie-Ann was wrapped in fur rugs, and placed in the sledge.

The dogs were restless to go, tails wagging. 'Yip! Yip!' called the mailman, and they sped off over the snow.

Carrie-Ann held on tightly at first, feeling scared. Soon, though, she was chatting excitedly, and finding the right letter at each stop.

When home again, the mailman carried her in. He laughed to Mummy, 'I think she's shamming, don't you?'

For Carrie-Ann's eyes were sparkling, and her cheeks the brightest red.

Ducks on ice

David was bored. He lived in a little village in the country and today his friend Andrew was to have visited him, but Andrew lived in an even smaller village and his mother had just rung up to say they were snowed in, so Andrew couldn't come.

'Why don't you go down to the pond and feed the ducks?' said David's mother. 'They'll need food in this weather. Take Skippy, he could do with a walk, but be careful of the ice on the pond.'

So David, and Skippy his dog, with a *huge* bag of bread walked down to the village pond. It looked quite magical. The water was frozen and the overhanging trees sparkled with icicles.

David spotted the ducks huddled together and Skippy saw them too. He went bounding over the ice. Suddenly his legs went 'splat' and he slithered forward on his tummy.

David couldn't help laughing. Poor Skippy looked so surprised and so funny. He felt much more cheerful and the poor cold ducks seemed happier too, eating big chunks of bread and fluffing up their feathers to keep themselves warm.

A magic city

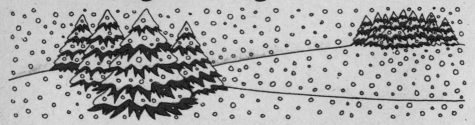

Kaye was staying with her Aunt Vivien and cousin Michael
in Montreal for Christmas and New Year. So far, she had
had a lovely time. Aunt Vivien and Michael had been so
kind that she hardly missed her father and mother back
home at all. But one thing she didn't like about Montreal
was the weather. She was not used to such bitter, finger-
numbing cold. It made her feel almost ill.

One day before Christmas, Aunt Vivien said, 'Come on
children. Let's go and get the last of our shopping.'

'Oh no, Auntie,' said Kaye, looking out of the window.
'It's so cold today, I can't bear to go out.'

'We'll go shopping somewhere where you won't have
to go out,' said Aunt Vivien. 'You won't even need a hat
or gloves.'

Ten minutes later they clambered into Aunt Vivien's car
and headed for the inner city. Suddenly, they swooped
down an underpass, made a few turns, and stopped in a
huge underground car park.

'Where are we?' said Kaye.

'Wait and see,' said Aunt Vivien and Michael.

They stepped into a lift. When the doors opened again
they were standing in the middle of a small street. There
were little shops on either side, a few pavement cafés, even
a fountain, and the whole street was covered with a high
roof! Kaye had never been anywhere like it. Other little

streets led off the main one, and everywhere people were shopping and drinking coffee outside the cafés as if it were a hot summer's day.

Aunt Vivien and Michael laughed at Kaye's amazement. 'Come on,' said Michael, 'let's get our shopping done, and then Mum will buy us an ice-cream soda each.'

An hour later they were sitting under a striped umbrella outside a café sipping huge ice-cream sodas. Kaye was still wide-eyed.

'It's only a shopping precinct,' said Michael laughing.

'Not to me,' said Kaye. 'It's like a magic city, where suddenly it's summer in the middle of winter.'

Snow and surf

Helen was very pleased when her aunt and uncle from Britain came to Australia for Christmas, bringing their daughter Sheila. Helen and Sheila were the same age, but this was the first time they'd met. They liked each other at once, and soon Helen was asking Sheila to tell her all about winter in Britain – and especially about snow.

Helen's family lived in a warm place near the sea, where it never snowed. Yet people in Britain, and some in Australia too, sent her Christmas cards with pictures of snowy landscapes and children throwing snowballs or building snowmen. But if you've never seen or touched real snow, it's very hard to imagine what it's like.

Sheila tried to explain. 'Well, it's very cold,' she said, 'and it makes your fingers tingle, and sometimes it sticks together in a ball, and sometimes it just crumbles in your hand. And when it thaws and melts, it goes all mushy and slushy and wet.'

Helen thought how lucky Sheila was, being able to throw snowballs and build snowmen and slide down hills on her sledge. But she still found it hard to imagine exactly what snow was like to touch and feel. 'Is it all white and frothy, like surf?' she asked.

'What is surf like?' asked Sheila. 'I've seen those pictures of big waves and people on surfboards, but I'd love to see real surf.'

'Then I'll show you!' said Helen. They ran down to the beach, and there they saw the surfers, balancing on their boards and riding in on the frothy, curling waves.

'Oh, that looks better than snow!' cried Sheila.

'We'll come down here for a beach picnic on Christmas Day,' said Helen.

Sheila was amazed at the thought of being out-of-doors
having a picnic on a sunny beach, at Christmas. 'You *are*
lucky!' she said.

'Yes, I suppose we are, really,' said Helen, 'but we don't
have any snow.'

'And *we* don't have any surf, where we live,' said Sheila,
'or Christmas picnics, either!'

'I've got an idea,' said Helen. 'Maybe we could take it in
turns to spend Christmas at each other's homes – that way,
we could have snow one year, and surf the next!'

'Great!' said Sheila, and they started to build a 'snowman',
out of sand.

Decorations

Julie and Charlie's father was an artist. One Christmas he took them shopping for decorations for their house. They looked all round a big store, but Julie and Charlie's father thought all the decorations were *very* expensive and he wasn't very rich. 'I know,' he said, 'we'll make our own decorations this year. First we'll visit the heath.'

When they got there they spent an hour picking sprays of gorse and holly and heather, collecting fir cones and even twigs. Then they visited a paint shop, where Father bought lots of little pots of paint.

When they arrived home Father spread newspaper all over the table and began to paint. Julie and Charlie helped him. They painted all the twigs gold and silver, the gorse was painted white and they just blobbed spots of all colours on the heather which looked rather funny but very pretty.

When the children's mother came home from work, she couldn't believe her eyes. 'Goodness, how lovely,' she said.

The carol singers

This year Mother had promised that Ned could go carol singing with his brothers and sisters. He was seven, the youngest of the family. His father called them his 'mini-choir'. Every year the family went carol singing in aid of a children's home in the small village where they lived.

When it was dark they set out around the village all wrapped up in their warmest clothes. The moon sparkled on the crisp snow and Father carried an old lantern which glowed brightly over them.

Everywhere they sang, people gave them money, and when they reached the old manor house Mrs Pemberton invited them all in. She took them all into the sitting room and gave them mince pies and roast chestnuts and muffins and mugs of chocolate.

'What a lovely way to earn money,' Ned thought.

A Christmas lamb

On the moors, farmers dread heavy snowfalls, because of the danger to their sheep.

One Christmas Eve, very late, Dick's father came into the kitchen from the farmyard. The snow on his coat melted in the warmth, and made puddles on the stone floor.

'I'm still a sheep missing,' he sighed, 'but I'd better have a bite, before I search again.'

Dick finished his soup in silence. His father was tired, he knew. Mother put out more soup, and Dick quietly slipped away. Outside, the wind bit into his face, and the snow stuck in his eyes.

'Come on Scamp,' he said to his dog. 'Let's go and find that poor sheep.'

It was a while before anyone realized Dick was missing. 'The stupid boy!' said his father, upset. 'Doesn't he know he can be buried – just like the sheep?' And he set off to fetch him back.

Dick was weary. The snow made walking difficult. But Scamp was full of enthusiasm, and urged Dick ahead.

Scamp found the sheep behind a boulder and barked excitedly. Dick sank down beside the ewe thankfully. 'Let's have you home, old girl,' he said, imitating his father. But she wouldn't move. Dick tugged and pulled, but the sheep stayed put.

Then Dick heard his father's voice, drifting through the snowflakes. 'Here, Dad!' he yelled.

His father rushed up, stumbling through the snow. 'So you found her?' he said, surprised.

'Scamp did,' said Dick. 'But look, she won't move!'

'I'll soon have her,' said Dad, then he scolded Dick, hard.

'But Dad, I wanted to help you.'

'Aye, but when you're older lad. Not this weather, nor this late hour.'

He took hold of the sheep, and lifted her up in strong arms. They both stared in wonder. For there, was a little tiny lamb.

'Well I never!' Dad exclaimed. 'We'd better get them back, quickly.'

'I'll keep the lamb warm,' said Dick.

'A while longer,' said his father, 'it would have been too late.'

In the distance, the church clock struck twelve, its chimes echoing over the hills.

'Merry Christmas!' said Dick, laughing.

His father turned and smiled at him. 'Merry Christmas, Son.'

Mother was at the door to greet them. 'Thank goodness you're safe!' she cried.

'Merry Christmas!' grinned Dick. And he handed her a present – a tiny, woolly lamb.

Summer in winter

'We're going abroad for Christmas!' announced Daddy, and he showed the children where Tenerife was, on a map. 'That's where we are going, and we're going by aeroplane,' he told Ian and Debbie.

Debbie gasped. 'But Father Christmas won't find us, all that way away!'

'Yes he will!' Mummy laughed.

When they set off, it was raining. It made driving to the airport difficult. But soon, they were climbing upwards into the sky.

'Look!' cried Ian, 'the clouds are below us, now!'

And when they landed, they walked out into brilliant, warm sunshine – wearing winter woollies and coats.

'It's summer in winter!' Daddy joked.

They passed banana trees, and orange groves, and everywhere grew brightly coloured flowers.

'But,' said Debbie staring around, 'it doesn't feel like Christmas.'

The next day was Christmas Eve. The hotel was decorated for Christmas. There was a huge Christmas tree in a corner, and the tinsel glittered strangely in the sunshine. The children ran past it in their swimsuits.

'Race you to the pool!' shouted Ian, and they dived into the blue water. Their parents stretched out on sun-beds, and by the evening, all the family were quite suntanned.

They had dinner at night, and Debbie wore her best sundress. There were crackers to pull, and music to dance to, and everyone was laughing and jolly. Suddenly, it did seem more like Christmas.

Carols were sung, and then it was time for bed.

'Hang up your stockings!' called Daddy.

'You bet!' said Ian, excitedly.

Mummy went to say goodnight. 'Where's your stocking?' she asked Debbie.

'Oh,' said Debbie, 'I didn't think I would bother.'

'Nonsense!' laughed Mummy. 'How can you have Christmas without a stocking?'

How indeed, thought Debbie, imagining how it would be in the morning without one. For Father Christmas would *never* find them here.

She lay listening to the sea, dashing on the rocks until she fell asleep.

Ian woke her, charging around the room. 'Look what I've got!' he called.

Debbie couldn't believe her eyes. Her stocking was full!

Mummy and Daddy came in. 'Merry Christmas!' There was hugging and laughing and paper tearing and presents.

And then Mummy said, 'Come on, both of you – on with your swimsuits! Today, we'll go in the sea!'

In hospital

It was Christmas Eve and little Simon was in hospital. He had broken his leg when he fell off a swing in the playground and now he was in plaster up to his knee. He didn't feel ill, but he was very sad when he thought of all the things he would be missing at home on Christmas Day.

That night he couldn't sleep. He tossed and turned in bed until he heard the clock strike twelve. Suddenly, the ward door opened. Simon sat up and so did the other three children in the ward. They hadn't been able to sleep either. In through the door walked Father Christmas carrying an enormous sack. He stopped at each bed and gave each child a pile of presents.

'Now,' said Father Christmas, when he had given out all the presents, 'you must all get off to sleep!'

When Simon woke up on Christmas Day he opened his

presents from Father Christmas. He had some felt pens and a pad of paper so that he could draw pictures in bed!

Then Dad and Mum and his sister Becky arrived. They had brought all their presents as well as Simon's so that they could all open them together just like they did at home. The ward was full of families, and all the nurses had tinsel sparkling in their caps.

There was a huge Christmas lunch and Mum had brought lots of dates and nuts and sweets for afterwards. In the afternoon everyone played games and at teatime there was a procession of small children from the local school dressed up as angels, each child carrying a candle. Simon knew that he might have been with them if he hadn't broken his leg and he was sad for a moment, but then he saw lots of his friends waving to him from under their wings and he wasn't sad anymore.

Then everyone grouped round the huge Christmas tree in the ward and sung carols. When Mum kissed Simon goodbye that evening she said, 'I hope it's not been a horrible Christmas, darling.'

'Oh no,' said Simon 'I've had a lovely time, although it will be nice to be at home again next year.'

Pantomime on ice

Alex and his little brother Jack, lived in a tiny village in the country and had never been to a big city. One Christmas their granny, who lived in London, invited Alex and Jack to come and visit her. They had a wonderful time seeing all the sights and on their last day in London Granny took them to see *Cinderella on Ice*. The boys had never even been to an ordinary pantomime before, but a pantomime on ice, well. . . .

As the performance began, the lights dimmed and the ice shimmered as beautiful Cinderella swished gracefully on. Alex and Jack sat spellbound. Everyone skated so easily and the costumes and the skates glittered under the lights.

When the fairy coach came on to the ice it glided to a halt very near the boys. They could see inside it very clearly and it looked quite real. Then as Cinders got in, it began to turn into a pumpkin. Little Jack just couldn't believe it.

When they went home the next day he kept looking at all the marrows and big vegetables in his father's garden to see if they were ready to turn into a fairy coach.

The zoo in winter

Johnny was born in January so for his birthday treat he usually went to the circus or to a pantomime but this year he decided to go to the zoo.

It had been snowing all night so that when he arrived at the zoo with his father the snow lay thick and white on the ground, although the sun was shining.

First they visited the polar bears. The polar bears loved the snow. One big, very furry bear kept sliding down a little hill. 'Just like me on my toboggan,' said Johnny.

The huge, fierce Siberian tigers loved the snow too. One of them just lay quietly basking in the sun.

The seals made everyone laugh. Their pond was frozen, and the big floppy animals kept pulling themselves on to the ice to sunbathe, but they were so heavy that the ice cracked and 'splash!' the surprised seals fell in the water!

Johnny felt sorry for the poor chimpanzees. They were all huddled together in a corner and their teeth were chattering. Father said this was just their way of talking but Johnny wasn't sure until one winked at him.

First-footing

Duncan and Kirsty were twins and they lived in Scotland. The Scots always celebrate New Year and this year Duncan and Kirsty were to be allowed to stay up until midnight to see the New Year in. It was a very special New Year too because their big brother Dougie was coming home from Australia where he worked on a sheep farm. The whole family – uncles, aunts, cousins and of course Grandad and Grandma – were spending New Year at the twins' house to welcome Dougie home.

'What time is he coming Mummy?' Kirsty asked for at least the tenth time that day.

'I've told you darling, I'm not sure. It depends when his boat gets in,' said Mummy.

As the day went by, everyone arrived at the twins' house – except Dougie. Duncan and Kirsty were getting very anxious.

'Don't worry bairns,' said Grandad. 'He'll come in time for New Year.'

The evening wore on. Everyone ate mountains of food and played funny games. The grown-ups talked about who was going to 'first-foot' them.

'Whatever's that?' asked Kirsty.

Grandma explained. 'It's an old custom where the first man through the front door after the clock strikes midnight has to be dark haired and to carry a piece of coal, or the household will have a year's bad luck.'

'Goodness,' exclaimed the twins, 'Uncle Angus better do it. He's got very dark hair.'

Everyone agreed and just before midnight Uncle Angus went out into the garden to wait for the clocks to strike. 'Boom, boom, boom, boom, boom, boom, boom, boom, boom, boom, boom, boom!' said the clock in the corner.

'Hurray,' cried everyone. 'Happy New Year.'

'Dougie didn't get back in time,' said Kirsty sadly. There was a bang on the door.

'There's Uncle Angus,' cried Duncan. He flung the door open and there stood – not Uncle Angus – but another dark haired man carrying a large piece of coal.

Duncan shrieked, 'It's Dougie, it's Dougie!' and everyone gathered round hugging and kissing as Dougie came in.

Father said, 'Well that'll certainly mean a good year.'

'It will indeed,' said Dougie, 'and I even brought the coal all the way from Australia for a little extra bit of luck.'

School freeze

This was the coldest winter for sixty years according to the weathermen. Ben and Alice could believe them. They looked out of their window on Monday morning to see the ground covered with a hard white frost. Their father's car looked white too although really it was bright yellow.

'I'll never get it started,' he said. 'I feel like staying in bed today and not going to work.'

'Oh, so do we,' said Ben and Alice. 'Let's not go to school. It's such a long way.'

'What nonsense,' said Mother. 'It's a few minutes walk, and school is lovely and warm, and your father *is* going to work.'

Dad made a face and winked at Ben and Alice, who laughed.

Mother walked the children to school to show that the cold was really nothing much, then hurried back home again. Ben and Alice settled in their classroom. It really was quite warm there.

As morning wore on though, the classroom began to get very cold and the children shivered.

'You're imagining it children,' said Miss Griffiths, their teacher, when they complained, but she too was getting very cold.

Suddenly Amy Holland screamed. 'Look,' she cried, 'there's water pouring under the door.'

There certainly was. Miss Griffiths led all the children out to the hall. All the other classes were coming in there too. The headmistress sent for Thomas the caretaker.

'What *has* happened?' she asked him.

'All the pipes have burst, I'm afraid,' he said.

'Well, the school will have to be closed for a few days,' said the headmistress, 'until the pipes are mended.' All the children cheered and yelled.

'Let's go and skate on the pond,' said Ben to Alice.

'I'm going to roast chestnuts,' said Amy Holland.

Even Miss Griffiths was secretly pleased. She thought that she would prepare some lessons at home while toasting her feet by the fire, and drinking lots of hot tea.

Only Pipkin the school cat was annoyed. He usually slept in the boiler room and now he would have to find somewhere else for a few nights.

The ski race

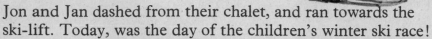

Jon and Jan dashed from their chalet, and ran towards the ski-lift. Today, was the day of the children's winter ski race!

Jon felt nervous. This was the first time he had joined the race. Soon, the lift was swinging them up the snowy peak. At the top, the other children were lining up, ready. Their ski-suits and woolly hats were bright against the whiteness.

'It isn't far,' said Jan, 'and look, some are smaller than you!'

Jon saw that even tiny children were there, and felt better. He and Jan checked their skis were fastened tightly.

'*Bang*!' went the starter, and with a whoosh and much laughing, the children flew downwards.

'See you!' yelled Jan, flashing past.

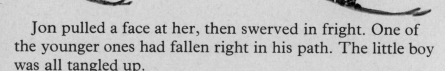

Jon pulled a face at her, then swerved in fright. One of the younger ones had fallen right in his path. The little boy was all tangled up.

Jon stopped with a shower of snow, and plodded back to him.

'Cheer up!' said Jon, putting him straight on his skis again. 'We'll race each other, instead!' So they set off down the slope again.

They arrived last.

'Goodness,' said Jan, 'I didn't realize you were *that* slow.'

The hungry reindeer

One winter's day Tarantus the reindeer was feeling very, very hungry. While he was out in the thick snow trying to find something to eat he met his brother Rudi. Rudi was looking fat and happy. He was pulling a sledge across the snow with a lot of parcels on it.

'Why don't you get a job pulling a sledge, like me?' said Rudi. 'I always get lots to eat in winter and never feel hungry.'

But Tarantus shook his head. 'I am a wild reindeer,' he said. 'I don't want to pull a sledge.'

'You will get very thin, then,' said Rudi. 'The snow has covered all the moss and lichen and wild bilberries.'

'I know what I will do,' said Tarantus. 'I shall travel to the big forest and eat conifer buds until the spring comes.' So Tarantus set off for the forest. It was a long way and he had to swim across an icy river. 'Oh, I do feel hungry,' he said, as he travelled across the snow in the darkness.

Tarantus reached the forest at last, and he saw bits of green showing, as the snow melted.

'Spring at last!' he said as he raced along. 'I shan't need to pull a sledge like Rudi after all.'

The stories in this book are by:
Gillian Denton Joan Eadington Judith Glover Janice Godfrey
Diane Jackman Daphne Lister Gillian Maxwell Janet Slingsby
Gordon Snell Jane Waller Freda Ward

The illustrations are by:
Glynnis Ambrus   David Barnett   Shirley Bellwood   Corrine Burrows
Lynne Byrnes   Jacky Cowdrey   David Eaton   Douglas Hall
Susan Hunter   Lisa Jensen   David Mostyn   Sandy Nightingale
John Patience   Peter Richardson   Jane Scott   Nancy Stephens
Tony Streek   Shirley Tourret

Cover illustration by John Patience

First published 1981 by The Hamlyn Publishing Group Limited
London · New York · Sydney · Toronto
Astronaut House, Feltham, Middlesex, England
© Copyright The Hamlyn Publishing Group Limited 1981

ISBN 0 600 36471 2

Printed in Italy